Anonymous

Half-hours with great authors

Anonymous

Half-hours with great authors

ISBN/EAN: 9783337281557

Printed in Europe, USA, Canada, Australia, Japan

Cover: Foto ©Andreas Hilbeck / pixelio.de

More available books at **www.hansebooks.com**

HALF-HOURS

WITH

GREAT AUTHORS,

WM. M. THACKERAY, T. B. MACAULAY,
BRET HARTE, THOMAS HOOD,
AND OTHERS.

CHICAGO AND NEW YORK:
BELFORD, CLARKE & CO.
1884.

CONTENTS.

A TREBLE TEMPTATION.

By the Author of " It is always too early to Sew," " Love me Tall, Love me Short," " Who's Griffiths ? " etc.

CHAPTER I.

IR CHARLES BUSSIT was,from an early age, subject to fits, but he inherited the Tuppennie Bussit Estates. Mr. Robert Bussit, his cousin, would have done so if Sir Charles hadn't. Hence Robert's hatred of Charles. Nothing more simple.

Sir Charles, being a gay young man, was on visiting terms with the beautiful La Dorchester. Becoming, suddenly, a marrying man, he fell deeply in love with Miss Isidora Spruce. Robert also loved her. This was an additional reason for his hating Sir Charles, and added fuel to the flame.

From this moment, Robert commenced writing anonymous letters to Isidora and her father. He wrote at least twenty a-day, signing them differently every time. Observing that the letters were taken in, but that the young lady and her father were not, he had recourse to other means.

He called on La Dorchester, who saw through him at once, played him adroitly, and then ordered him out of the house.

This was his third reason for hating his cousin.

He now took to shouting through the keyholes and windows of Sir Alexander Spruce's house defamations of Sir Charles's character.

These energetic means, at last, had their effect.

Sir Charles being refused admittance, had a succession of fits on the doorstep. He was told to move on by a policeman, and was rescued from his painful situation by La Dorchester in her ponychaise, who thenceforth took the matter in her own hands.

Robert was now delighted, and, on the strength of the probability of the Tuppennie Bussit Estates coming to him, bought a secondhand brass doorplate, with somebody else's name on it.

Sir Charles Bussit got over his fits, and came out stronger than ever.

This sent up Robert's hatred to fever heat.

It was evident that the Tuppennie Bussit Estates had slipped from his grasp for this once.

Then he waited.

But while he waited, La Dorchester acted

CHAPTER II.

ISIDORA SPRUCE was the daughter of Commander-in-Chief Spruce, a retired veteran much beloved by his officers and men, as a genuine martinet of the old school. So much was he beloved, that when he retired, the entire army retired with him. This led to complications and subsequent alterations in the Purchase System.

Isidora was a blonde, tall and *mince*, with gentle blue wondering eyes, of about the middle height, with dark brown tresses, and rather inclined to that sort of *embonpoint* which is the sure sign of gentle descent.

She was always saying, "*May* I?" in a plaintive tone, which caused her to be a favorite with every one.

To this her fond doting father had but one answer, "No. you mayn't," which evinced the deep sympathy existing between the parent and child.

"*May* I marry Sir Charles Bussit?" she asked, one morning, as they were seated together on a *canapé de luxe*, breakfasting lightly ; "*May* I ? "

" No, you mayn't," answered the Commander-in-Chief, his eyes filling with the moisture which so often accompanies the sudden deglutition of over-caloricated bohea.

" May I give him up? " she inquired, playfully, " *May* I ? "

" No, you mayn't," replied the Warrior.

That was all she wanted. She had gained her point, and so, tapping him lightly on the head with a bootjack, which she had been embroidering for his especial use, she glided from the room.

" Two persons wanted to see his Commander-in-Chief-ship," a servant said. " Might they enter? "

" No, they mightn't," returned the Veteran. So they came in.

It was Sir Charles's solicitor, Mr. Slyboots, and La Dorchester.

The Commander-in-Chief motioned them to a chair. They took two, and seated themselves. So far all was well.

Then what happened?

Why, La Dorchester, with a woman's ready wit,

introduced the old Solicitor to the old Warrior, **and** the Solicitor, with the cunning of his craft, answered to his cue, and introduced La Dorchester to **the** Commander-in-Chief.

"Mr. Slyboots,"—La Dorchester said.

The Commander-in-Chief bowed.   So did **Mr.** Slyboots.

"La Dor"—commenced Slyboots, courteously.

"—Chester," said the Lady, brusquely.   **Then** they sat still and wondered.

CHAPTER III.

N two minutes the Veteran was put in possession of The Facts. This was owing entirely to the female tact and ready wit. She went to the point at once, while Slyboots, with professional routine, would have read precedents, habendum clauses, and the history of Nisi Prius before coming to the object of their visit. He had prepared himself with documents. Before he had got them all arranged on the table, from which he was obliged to sweep the Sèvres cups, saucers, urn and spirit-lamp, La Dorchester had stated the case. She exculpated Sir Charles.

Isidora had expected these visitors, and, Love being capable of meannesses, had concealed herself within hearing.

The Veteran suspected as much, and saw through La Dorchester's plan. He quietly moved the ormolu fire-screen to the front of the grate.

By this movement of the old Campaigner La Dorchester was unexpectedly checkmated.

Then she told her story, and Slyboots listened, legal documents in hand, dismayed.

He would have stopped her had it been in his power, but perceiving, with the true instinct of an old student of Barnard's Inn, that this was not possible, he carefully adjusted the red tape on the sixty parchments he had brought with him, and sat silent, with *Blackstone* on his knee, for warmth.

"Hush, Madam! not so loud, please," whispered the Commander-in-Chief, looking uneasily towards the chimney.

"WHY NOT?" bawled his beautiful visitor, at the top of her voice. LISTENERS NEVER HEAR NO GOOD OF THEMSELVES, DO THEY?"

With this the bold woman rose suddenly from her chair, and, spurning the drugget, dashed at the poker, seized it, and upset the ormolu screen.

"May I?" said a sweet voice from about two yards up the chimney.

"No, you mayn't," returned the Veteran.

But she could not control herself, and gliding downwards, fell at La Dorchester's feet, her head on her outstretched hands.

Isidora, from her well-chosen place of concealment, had heard every syllable. She was prostrated, writhing, blackened. For this last she cared little. Soot blackens faces, not characters ; this they well knew, and felt it.

The Commander-in-Chief was the first to speak and break the silence.

He addressed La Dorchester.

" For shame, Madam ! " said the Commander-in-Chief. Whereupon both women began to cry.

Then the Commander-in-Chief looked at the Solicitor, and the Solicitor looked at himself in a glass, and himself in a glass looked at Isidora, who, in her turn, looked at La Dorchester.

They all sighed deeply, and said nothing.

In another second La Dorchester was on her legs, giving eloquent screams.

" He loves you still ! " said the Solicitor, vaguely. It is in some natures to be vague, and his was one of those natures. Otherwise he was a clever man.

CHAPTER IV.

IVE weeks after this the bells of Tuppennie Bussit Church rang out a merry peal. The ringers had practised triple bob majors, two bobs, bobs and tizzies, bobs and benders, and other varieties of the ringer's art, until they were perfect in the first two bars of the *Dead March in Saul.* This once mastered, they gave way with a will.

Then came ten outriders, ushered by six hussars, each bearing a banner with a motto, and followed by a van covered with pictures of celebrated fat women, the Giant of Norfolk, the Lion Tamer, and the Battle of Trafalgar in oils and distemper.

Then there was a loud cheer from the steeple, which, getting quite shaky with excitement, tried to come down and join the throng. Presently several Spiritualistic mediums, specially engaged for the occasion, floated about the top of Bussit House, waving flags. Murmurs. Cheers. Tears. Horses heard in the distance. More distance, more horses. Bussit gates flung open, and keepers, grooms, peasants, cooks, housekeepers, butlers, footmen and pages, all clustering about on each other's shoulders, and hanging in festoons from the heights of the ancient portals.

Then more outriders, riding outside their horses, boldly. Then a troop of less daring horsemen, who, fearing the shouts of the crowd, had got inside, and pulled the blinds down. Then came the carriage itself, drawn by twenty wild horses in front, and pushed up behind by as many more of the same breed. The drag was down, but they dashed through the little village, amid roars of delight from the millions that had congregated to witness this great event.

The carriage was open, and in it sat Sir Charles and Isidora: she quite blinded the sun's rays with her beauty, so much so that some elderly people, more knowing than the rest, got out smoked glasses to look at her, and others, not so learned, thought the whole affair was an eclipse, and went home to write to the local papers.

"*May* I?" she said.

Her husband smiled assent. and, rising from her

seat, she leapt on to the nearest horse's back, and performed several feats of horsemanship, which raised the enthusiasm of the spectators to an unprecedented pitch.

Robert Bussit saw, and the sight thrilled him. Catching his eye, she quivered for an instant; but in another second she was back, at a single bound, clearing fifty-five feet upwards, and downwards, and into her husband's carriage, scattering largesse to the crowd around.

Then they swept into the Mansion, smiling, capering, laughing, screaming, through files of retainers in every sort of varied costume, radiant with squibs, crackers, and Catherine-wheels in their button-holes, with which they made a fine display, and Isidora thought no more of Robert Bussit, than a bright Bird of Paradise thinks of last year's boots.

But Birds of Paradise can't be always thinking of boots; and boots, with something living in them, may rise up, thick-soled, and kick, until the Bright Creature feels the pain, shudders, droops, and falls into the dust.

CHAPTER V.

OBERT BUSSIT, acting upon the advice of Sniffkin, his friend and solicitor, had married a pale-faced wife. She was the daughter of one of Sniffkin's clients, and had conceived a gentle admiration for Robert's *torso*. His *torso*, and his color, which was a brightish red, like sunset on a carrot, with just the slightest suspicion of green in the left eye. pleased her. She had fifty thousand pounds, nominally to provide her with a trousseau, and this excited Robert Bussit's admiration.

It was simply *Trousseau* caught by *Torso*, or *vice versâ* if you will.

When Molly Borne, to whom Robert had artfully promised himself some time before, heard the bells ringing for this wedding, she writhed all over Tuppennie Bussit house, like an injured basilisk. On the evening of Robert's wedding she stood by his back gate and threw stones at him. He then saw that for this woman his *torso* had no power. Then

he admired her.   But this feeling gave way to fear :
the Hater was confronted by a Hatred, strong, un-
relenting, as his own.

Within a year of this union of Torso with Trousseau, the bells of Tuppennie Bussit church rang again.

This time they announced the first appearance of
a small Robert Bussit, and Robert Bussit, *père*, was
all over the place with prideful joy.

It was all Boy with him now.   His doubts were
developing into certainties.   His hopes boy'd him
up, and so inflated did he become, that, but for his
friend Sniffkin and a couple of stout ropes, he would
have risen, balloon-like, floated over the house-top,
and have been lost.

But Sniffkin couldn't afford to lose so valuable a
client.   Hence his method.

After a time he calmed down.

Then the Hater came well to the front.   He built
a tower sixteen hundred feet high, by five in circum-
ference, with a sort of tank at the top, roofed in, and
pierced with large windows, whence he could command a Birdseye view of the entire Tuppennie Bussit
estates.   Here he and Mrs. Bussit, with the Future
Heir in Sniffkin's arms, would sit taking tea and
shrimps on a summer's evening.

Here it was his delight to point out to the child all that should be his in prospect.

This tower he called the *Tower of Teazer.*

From here he could throw cups and saucers down on Sir Charles and Lady Bussit's heads as they took their evening walk.

They wondered at first where they came from. After a time they ceased to wonder.

All this began to have an effect on a man naturally irritable. Sir Charles *was* naturally irritable. In addition, Robert Bussit grew a magnificent mustache. It was the talk of the whole place. This his cousin had never been able to accomplish. Robert now appeared with a beard perfectly Oriental and a profusion of long glossy hair. Sir Charles and Lady Bussit became aware of his head and face one day, thrust out at them, over the top of a hedge.

Lady Bussit saw and sighed. This chafed the Hairless man. He tried extra shaving, but cut himself severely. Smarting under his wound Sir Charles spoke unkindly to his wife. Lady Bussit bore all with resignation. Let this be remembered to her credit.

Then little, meek, pale Mrs. Bussit, at the instigation of her husband, let down her back hair, and displayed it over the tower. It reached nearly half-way to the ground.

Lady Bussit had nothing of her own but a chignon. Sir Charles couldn't assist her. Then they both, avoiding one another, and taking different ways, would wander down into the village, and stand gazing into the barbers' windows, where there were lifelike block heads with Circassian hair. This constant pining produced an effect purely physical on Lady Bussit.

She moulted.

Sir Charles gradually became bald.

One day, in his justice room, he sentenced a gipsy for stealing a hare. The woman was led out wailing and protesting her innocence. It was on Robert Bussit's evidence, and a murmur of applause went through the justice room, when the people saw his splendid *torso* and glorious locks, mustache and beard. Lady Bussit was, on these magisterial occasions, accommodated with a seat on the bench in the study. Robert walked out. Husband and wife were alone. She threw herself at his knees. " O Charles ! can such things be ? "

Then he tried to comfort her, but could not, and the Hairless ones wept together.

CHAPTER VI.

OBERT BUSSIT had seen, heard, and had taken to thinking.

The result of his cogitation was soon obvious.

It was this.

There could be no doubt that Sir Charles was mad. The French have their expression for his madness, we have not. *Fou comme un chabelier.* What was to be done?

Robert Bussit took counsel with his old friend Sniffkin.

Sniffkin saw the difficulty, and touched it.

Sir Charles's sanity hung on a single hair. On consideration it was evident that he was only fit for one place.

The Zoological Gardens.

But how to get him there?

Sniffkin explained technically

Robert Bussit was not in a humor for technicalities.

"For heaven's sake, man," he cried, "tell me HOW to do it, and I'll do it."

Sniffkin calmed him down by tickling him under the left ear, and then, quietly lighting a cigar, explained his method.

It was necessary to obtain three magistrates' orders and a certificate of improper vaccination. That was all.

Robert Bussit slept soundly that night, for he saw his way, at last, clear to the Tuppennie Bussit estates.

In the morning he and Sniffkin swore the necessary information, and before two o'clock Sir Charles was safely locked up with the bears.

At three he was fed.

The next day people brought him buns, and he amused himself by climbing up the pole. There was no way of escape; he saw *that*, and submitted.

Finding himself in this situation, he made friends as best he could with his companions, and their eccentricities began to interest him.

In the mean time the other side was not idle.

CHAPTER VII.

OLLY BORNE saw her mistress's distress, and whispered in her ear insidiously.

At this whisper Lady Bussit's eyes flashed fire, then she became preternaturally calm, and sent for the Curate.

Now, when a woman so gentle as Lady Bussit becomes preternaturally calm, and sends for a Curate, it means something.

The curate, Mr. Banjo, came and had an interview with Slyboots, the Family Solicitor.

Slyboots was of opinion, five times, that nothing could be done. This amounted, ultimately, to one pound thirteen and fourpence, besides expenses in coming down from London.

The Curate left Slyboots in the dining-room, where he continued giving his opinion to the cold chicken, tongue, and viands on the table from mere force of habit, and putting it down at six and eightpence, every time, in his pocket-book.

Lady Bussit thanked Mr. Banjo, the Curate, for his prompt attention to her summons.

Mr. Banjo blushed and clasped his hands.

" I would do anything for you. * * * Lady Bussit," he said, and sat down, nervously, on a workbox, among the needles, by accident.

Lady Bussit was too much absorbed to notice the young man's agitation.

" Let us come to the point," she said.

" I have," murmured Mr. Banjo, removing the last and sharpest needle.

Then they sat opposite one another, and fixed their eyes sadly on the carpet.

" Slyboots is too slow, too timid," said Mr. Banjo ; "*I* would *act*, and at once."

" How ? "

" We require a man of superhuman genius."   Mr. Banjo blushed as he said this, slightly turned to the right, then he went on. " We require a man of unbounded energy,"—he blushed again, and turned slightly to the left—" a man, handsome as Apollo, strong as Hercules, clever as Minerva, with the will of Jove, and the pluck of Mars."   His face was suffused with blushes.

Lady Bussit caught some of his enthusiasm.

"You are describing *Yourself*," she exclaimed, her whole face beaming with admiration of the athletic form before her.

"Not so," returned the Curate, gently; "I spoke of another; though," he added, diffidently, "I felt at the moment you would recognize the portrait in *me.* It was natural," and once more he blushed, this time deeply.

"Then where is there such a person?"

"I know."

"Who?"

"He is a Writer, an Author, of whose stupendous genius there are no two opinions,* even among his enemies, for enemies he has; no truly great man can exist without making them. Everybody is raving about him, everywhere. His friends rank him next after Homer, and far above Shakspeare. Even his enemies are forced to admit him to an equal pedestal with our greatest Dramatic Poet. He never writes

---

*The character which the Curate here describes, and which will shortly be before my readers in these pages, is no fictitious one, but a portrait, a speaking likeness, of the writer of this novel. Vandyck drew a full length of himself, so did Rubens, so Salvator Rosa and Raphael, Quentin Matsys carved himself in iron on the top of a pump; and not to multiply instances, an eminent novelist has, in our own time, given an admirable sketch of himself; so why should not *The Author of this Novel*?

but to defend the cause of the weak and helpless.
His works teem with all the Christian virtues.   The
number of people that have been converted by merely reading the titles on the covers of his books,
would alone form a small London Directory.   He is
thoroughly in earnest.   There is his secret ; and being so, has already contrived to get several people
both *into* and *out* of, the Zoological Gardens."

"Is it possible?   Let us go to him."

"I will write, and make an appointment with him."

"Do.   A writer?   What does he write?"

"Everything."

After an instant's thought she replied, "Indeed !
Then I am acquainted with many of his works."

The Curate sailed over the carpet like an antelope,
and approached his lips to her ear.   He whispered,
"He writes for *P—nch*."

At the mention of this name a thrill of ecstatic pleasure ran through her frame.   Then, recovering herself
wtih a strong effort, she exclaimed, joyfully, "Do not
delay an instant.   *He is evidently the friend we need.*"

Mr. Banjo went into the study, and dispatched
his note to Mr. Juff, the celebrated Author.   Then
Mr. Banjo came down again, looking flushed and
handsome.   Then he blushed.

CHAPTER VIII.*

EXT morning in came Mr. Banjo. Glowing with health and high spirits, the Athlete crashed through the conservatory window, and stood before Lady Bussit. "Coo!" said the gentle Curate. Whereat Lady Bussit raised her head, and listened.

"Shall I read you Juff's letter?" he asked.

"You shall."

"*'Dear Sir,—The case of a gentleman confined in the Zoological Gardens among the bears, by an interested relative, is a first-rate notion, and looks like truth. There is matter in it for a novel, a drama, a poem, ultimately a burlesque, and at Christmas time a pantomime. Let the lady call on me in person. Perhaps I can get her an engagement in London, or the provinces,*

---

* "The length of this chapter is exceptional, but so is its subject. I have attempted to portray the author of this novel—myself. It has been a delicate task, but I think I have succeeded."—*Extract from Author's Letter to the Editor.*

*where, by the way, she might "star" in a play of mine
on this very subject. At home every day, and to
special visitors at any hour, if you touch the little ivory
knob on the right side of my door, one foot from the
step. As for you, I know you. You pulled No. 6 in
the University Fours at Henley, and took a threepenny
'bus, instead of a cab. from the Marble Arch to the
Haymarket, to save ninepence. See " Ride Journal,"
April 1, cited in my " Joke Book," same date, and also
in my " Indices Subjicientes Spectacula, Comædias, et
Ludicra," under " B " for " Banjo."*

　　　　　　　　　" ' Yours very heartily,

　　　　　　　　　　　　" ' JUFF.' "

"And did you?"

"Did I what?"

"Save ninepence?"

"Yes."

"How noble and how bold you are!"

Banjo blushed all over.　It took him exactly three
minutes to do this, and unblush again.

Then he resumed :—

"You'll call on Mr. Juff."　She hesitated, and he
continued.　"He won't come down here.　A marvel-
lously popular writer, like Juff, is spoiled by the
ladies.　They won't let him alone.　They pet him,

play with him, write to him, dance round him, in
crowds, all day long. So you can't expect him to
come down here on a stranger's business."

Lady Bussit decided to go, took her maid, Molly
Borne, with her, and travelling by the Unlimited
Express from Bussit Station, was at Mr. Juff's door
by half-past exactly.

It was a magnificent house in the finest quarter of
Belgravia.

Its site had been formerly a square, but had been
purchased (out of the receipts from one of his papers
in *P–nch*), by Mr. Juff, whose quick eye had at once
seized upon its capabilities.

Chestnuts, oaks, Scotch firs, and the African pine,
so rarely seen in the metropolis, stood between the
busy thoroughfare and Mr. Juff's front door.

There were two entrance lodges, which were gems
of the best architectural design, and the drive was
divided from the pathway by a narrow but clear
running stream, whereon a gondola was in waiting
to convey such visitors as might prefer this mode of
arriving at the house.

Lady Bussit could not conceal her admiration and
wonder at all she saw. She had been reared in the
idea that authors lived on airy flights, in Bohemia,

not Belgravia, and this palace—for it was no less
—astonished her.

At first she thought she must have made a mistake ; but the name " Juff " over the lodges, on the
gate-pillars, on the gravel of the tramway, on the
tesselated pavement (where it was inlaid with costly
stones), and on the prow and flag of the gondola, at
once dissipated any such idea.

A slave, black as ebony, suddenly stood before
her, and facing round, led the way to the Italian por
tico.

At the front door she called to mind Mr. Juff's
own instructions, and pointed to the small ivory
knob.

The negro pressed it lightly. He then respectfully salaamed and, drawing himself up to his full
height, disappeared.

There was no time allowed Lady Bussit for speculation on this new wonder, for the hall-door, mov-
ing noiselessly, and apparently of its own accord,
stood open before her.

She summoned up all her resolution, repeating to
herself several times, " Charles,—Husband,—Zoological Gardens."

" *May* I ? " she asked timidly of nobody. She

was standing on a door mat of the purest Circassian tresses, prepared after some occult receipt.

Silence assents. There was no answer. She advanced a step, and the hall door closed.

So noiselessly was this done, and so admirably did the door fit into the wall, that neither sound nor seam could show her where she had entered.

The hall was of Basilica pattern, lighted round the dome by some thousands of rose-colored lanterns which, entirely hidden from sight, shed warm and cheering bloom upon the interior. Frescoes by the greatest masters of the Italian school, rendered the dome glorious and illustrated the chief events of Mr. Juff's career.

Accustomed to the grandest houses, Lady Bussit was utterly overwhelmed by these simple, but artistic effects.

Then it struck her that it was either all a dream, or that she had gone into St. Peter's at Rome by mistake.

" Well, I NEVER ! ! " exclaimed Molly.

This observation recalled Lady Bussit to herself. She now became aware of a fragrant aromatic breeze pervading the Hall. This seemed to refresh her, and she approached the fountain which was musically splashing in the centre. This was so contrived that every single drop of water from the jet fell upon a peculiarly-fashioned stone, and gave forth such varied sounds as produced a harmony, the like of which Lady Bussit had never heard.

In the centre of the fountain now appeared a lovely maiden habited like a Naiad, who, presenting an oyster shell made of rare Indian pearl enshrined in gold, chased by Benvenuto Cellini, bade Lady Bussit note her name and business upon it with an electric pencil. She thought a few lines, which were suddenly reproduced in writing on the shell, which she forthwith returned to the maiden, who instantly disappeared, while soft music penetrated the air. Turning her head towards the quarter whence these sounds came, she perceived a beautiful Indian girl motioning her to follow.

She did so. Not a sound of London could be heard. Not the roll of an omnibus, not the rattle of a cab, not the footfall of a policeman. Yet, this was Belgravia.

At the maid's touch two huge glass doors flew open. These disclosed a Tropical grove. Mangoes, cocoa-nuts, oranges, hung in clusters. Birds of the brightest plumage and most enchanting song fluttered hither and thither, cooling the air by the fan-like motion of their gorgeous wings.

Parrots had built in the sycamores, and were teaching their young to speak such words as they themselves had learnt.

They had one or two varieties of cry. The sounds that Lady Bussit caught were " Juff," " The Great Juff," " Juff's at home." So she passed on.

More glass doors, which opening, showed, as it were, the Depths of the Ocean.

Here fish disported themselves, and Lady Bussi and her maid walked on a carpet of the finest sand through stalactite caves, cool crystal grots, and beneath arches of flowering seaweed trees.

Then they were ushered into a Hall of more than· Peruvian splendour.

Masterpieces of painting and sculpture surrounded her. A soft clear light was diffused through the apartment. Mirrors dexterously let into the walls reflected, noiselessly, the outside world, and pictured as it were, the most beautiful spots in the London Parks, showing how adroitly the Designer had fixed the site of his residence.

So far all was romantic: but in a corner, beneath a palm tree, stood a writing table, and over various doors, which Lady Bussit now noticed for the first time, were written "Tragedies," "Comedies," "Novels," "Romances," "Burlesques," "Magazines," and other inscriptions, which she could not at once understand.

By the writing table were huge baskets of gold, silver and iron. These were labelled, severally, Jokes, Good Things, Repartees, Impromptus, Plots, Puns, Used, Unused.

For Mr. Juff was not one of those writers who trust to the Inspiration of the Moment for success. He held that a good thing, once said, no matter by whom, ought never to be thrown away and lost, but catalogued and classed for reference, so as to be found when wanted.

Lady Bussit had barely time to form some idea of The Stupendous Genius which had done all this, when a bevy of laughing damsels, pelting with choice flowers some object at present hidden from her sight, entered the room.

"Our game is over," said a sweet voice, apparently from the Rosery whence the girls had issued. " Go to your ices. We will meet anon."

The ladies wandered away in various directions: and were soon lost to sight and hearing.

Then The Author, who had been enjoying a moment's recreation, approached the open window.

He was tall, classically handsome, and wore a suit of bright orange velvet turned up with blue ; his *mauve* shirt, made of a material unknown in this country, was fastened at the throat by one magnificent diamond.   His delicately chiselled hands peeped out, small and white, from the ruffles of the real point lace with which his wristbands were trimmed.

His shoes were of a rich crimson, which afforded an admirable setting for the amethysts, rubies, and smaller diamonds with which they were bespangled.

He was smoking a delicately-perfumed cigarette, and playing a mandoline, as he entered the room and stood before them.

CHAPTER IX.

ADY BUSSIT was agitated.

Mr. Juff saw this at once, and touched a spring in the wall. Thence issued a small silver salver, bearing an ancient beaker. He touched another spring just above. Thence flowed out a liquid bright and sparkling. . With this he filled the beaker, and handed it to Lady Bussit.

"*May* I ?" she inquired, faintly.

"Certainly. It will not hurt you. It is simply *Allsopina*. If it was Bass I should say something about *Basso profondo*.

Saying this he turned to one of his buckets, then to a large ledger, and made a formal entry under the letter B. The book was labelled "*Good things to say*." He then referred to a quarto index, which was standing, open, on a gothic brazen eagle near the writing-table. In this he made a private mark, for reference, also under letter B ; and this being done, he turned to attend to his visitor.

Then she told him all.

Mr Juff appeared to be thinking intently.

The result was soon apparent.

" How are you ? " he inquired,

She glanced at her maid.

Mr. Juff was on the alert in an instant, and spring-
ing from his chair, placed himself, at one bound, between them.

" Now then," he cried, " No larks: I want the
truth." Then he repeated, " How are you ? "

Lady Bussit paused. Reflecting, however, that
she could gain nothing by concealment, she replied,
" Pretty well, thank you ; how are you ? "

Mr. Juff thus challenged, begged a moment's delay.
Then he put his hands into his pockets and drew
forth a pair of shining bones. On these he performed several sonatas. After he had finished, this
strange romantic creature danced a saraband, and
then pushing forward from a corner a small rostrum
made of cedar wood inlaid with gold and ivory, he
mounted it, and addressed them.

" Lady Bussit and Maid, your husband is locked
up in the Zoological Gardens. From what I have
heard, I gather that loss of hair has affected his brain.
He has become light-headed. Robert Bussit thinks

this an opportunity for confining his cousin, and putting him under lock and key." He reflected for an instant, and then descending, rushed to his folio labelled " Jokes," wherein he made a note under the letter H, " *Hair. . . Locks . . . double meaning.*" Then he wrote a reference in his index. After this he resumed his position.

" This misfortune has reacted upon *you.* I have eyes and see it. The question simply is, *Do you want luxuriant hair, whiskers and mustachios?* Don't be alarmed. You sha'n't be like Julia Pastrana, a very amiable young lady with whom I have the pleasure to be acquainted." Here he kissed the tips of his fingers, and then continued. "No; you shall not even be compelled to dye." Here he dashed down again, and made another couple of entries under the letter " D—*Die—Dye*"—for future use, while Lady Bussit watched him with anxious interest. Gradually she came to respect his manliness, his courtesy, and to admire and understand his brilliant genius. He went on, " We will bide our time. In a week you will be ready to act. So will Sir Charles, to whom you shall convey a receipt with which I will furnish you."

" How great ! how clever you are !"

"I am. But, as the French say, *cela va sans dire.* Let us fix our attention on the one point. Leave all to me. When you feel that the moment has come, merely drop me a line, saying ' *Hair you ready ! If so go a-head.'* I shall then *act.* By the way, what is the name of the man who feeds the bears at three o'clock ? "

Lady Bussit thought for an instant. Then she replied, " Smith."

Mr. Juff turned to his index, and under the letter " S " found the name required.

"Good," he said, " he comes of an old French family. Now listen to me. I know how to deal with Smith. Smith is a snob. Go to the Zoological in State. Outriders, trumpets, flags, you understand."

" I do. I've got them all."

Juff bounded into the air with a loud cry, " Eureka ! Hooray ! Bravo ! My ! Here we are again ! How are you to-morrow ! See what I've found !" he shouted, like an elephant in an ecstasy.

Lady Bussit clasped her hands with joy. Electric fire coursed through her veins. She caught his enthusiasm. So did Molly. With a wild triumphant roar they all three sprang from their seats, and joining hands, bounded about the room. Guns went off in the ante-room, and jubilant music on hidden organs pealed forth a victorious chorus.

Then they cooled down, and Mr. Juff stamping his foot, the floor opened, and therefrom arose an elegantly-served table, bearing upon its marble top, gooseberries stuffed with cream, and iced flounders.

He made both mistress and maid drink a bottle of Pommery & Gréno's driest champagne each.

Then he wrote the receipt to be given to Sir Charles. Then he wished them good-day.

After this he measured three paces, carefully, backwards. Then running six forward, he stretched out his hands, and with a tremendous impetus, jumped through a small square window in the wall, about six feet from the floor. On his disappearance the window was immediately covered with a large flap on which was printed NOT AT HOME. Taking the hint, they withdrew.

As Lady Bussit passed into the street she heard behind her a tremendous bang, and then a roar which startled her.

It was Mr. Juff letting off a pun and laughing at it himself, for he was hard at work on a pantomime for Christmas, and their visit had disturbed him. Now he was returning to his toil.

ADY BUSSIT, acting upon instructions, appeared before the gate of the Zoological Gardens with outriders dressed in scarlet and pink. They had white hats turned up with blue, and yellow boots. A dozen running footmen accompanied the carriage, dressed as Tritons, and blowing conchs.

All this was not without its effect on Smith.

On the pretence of asking him at what time the bears were fed, she slipped a thousand-pound note into his hand, and a letter for Sir Charles.

This was duly delivered. Juff's receipt she put inside a bun, and threw it over the railings. Sir Charles seized it and devoured its contents. Then he nodded, passed his finger over his bald head thoughtfully, jotted something on the letter, and replacing it in the bun threw it playfully up to Lady Bussit. Thenceforward he was cheerful and resigned. The bears amused him with their absurdities.

They were all mad. One bear thought he was on the Stock Exchange, and showed Sir Charles a plan for rigging the market. The plan was marked methodically, A, B, C, D, etc., and the poor animal imagined himself a bear of Consols.

Sir Charles saw at once that *he* would never get out.

But from their conversation he learnt something which was ultimately of signal service to him.

They confided to him their secret griefs.

One, a she-bear, informed him that she would not have been there but for the wickedness of a barber in the city, who loved her, though she hated him, and who had paid Smith to fatten her up, and if he could not possess her alive, he would, by Smith's help, obtain her hand, and herself entirely, when dead.

Sir Charles passed his hand over his hairless scalp, and meditated.

Five days later the she-bear was removed. Smith informed Sir Charles of her destination. And now he was really anxious for his delivery.

Juff, too, wondered at the delay.

At last there came a note. " *Hair you ready ? Go a-head!* " Then Juff went to work.

He called on a manager of a metropolitan theatre.

The manager had just got together, with some trouble, a "double company" for Mr. Juff's forthcoming pantomime.

He also took the precaution of securing five large pantomime heads with various expressions of countenance. To wear these, he engaged four artists accustomed to this sort of work.

The fifth mask they carried.

Thus armed, Juff went to the Zoological.

The men with the large heads, being taken for distinguished foreigners, were received by the authorities, who showed them over the gardens with the greatest possible respect.

This drew the officials and the visitors away from the bears'-den.

Smith and another keeper came out to feed the bears.

The second keeper wheeled a barrow before him, in which was the bears' meat.

At a signal from Juff, the first clown and pantaloon engaged Smith in an animated conversation.

Obeying another sign, the second pair of panto. mimists stopped the barrow, and commenced tasting and bargaining for the meat.

From Smith's pocket, Clown number one **extracted**
the keys.

The man, missing these, turned upon him.

Then the clown, with the utmost politeness, pro-
tested, on his honor, with his hand at his heart,
that he could not be guilty of such a fraud, and
pointed to his companion, who had already run away,
as the culprit. The keeper strode off in search of
the latter.

In the mean time similar manœuvres had been executed by the other *artistes*, and the under-keeper
was in full chase of the second pantaloon, who he
supposed, had filched several pounds weight of the
fattest meat.

The first clown handed the keys to Mr. Juff.

Then the two drolls engaged themselves upon a
work of marvellous cunning.

They divided the fat purloined from the barrow,
and with two lumps of this stuff, they scrubbed the
walks of the Gardens, as if they were housemaids,
cleaning a floor.

In the mean time, Juff had descended, opened the
cage, released Sir Charles, placed the spare large
head on his shoulders, and thus disguised, he led

him by the grass borders, and, avoiding the paths, to the gate.

So far all was satisfactory.

But the alarm had been given.

Smith and the other keeper, finding themselves deceived, shouted out to the officials, who attempted to secure their large-headed visitors. This led to a scrimmage.

The clowns and pantaloons threw about everything they could find.

The police outside, hearing the noise, rushed in, and would have joined the affray, but for the precautions taken by the two clowns, who had rendered the walks so slippery with lard, that no one was able to stand upright for one second.

Then followed a scene of indescribable confusion, taking advantage of which, Juff and Sir Charles drove off, safely, in a cab.

In a few minutes, Lady Bussit held him, panting, shouting and dancing, in her arms.

It was a pretty picture.

Then Juff went home to work.

CHAPTER XI.

LADY BUSSIT was the first to speak.

"May I?" she asked.

"You may," was his reply.

Then she produced first of all Juff's receipt and the note added by Sir Charles.

She accounted for her delay by showing that the *Perruquier* to whom she had applied could not have performed his work quicker under the circumstances.

It was to be a temporary arrangement.

Juff's receipt had simply said,

"*Measure round the head in manner of a fillet, classically.*"

"*From the forehead over to the poll, electioneeringly.*"

"*From one temple to the other, religiously.*"

"*Write result down in inches. Your wife will apply it to a photograph, and the thing is done.*"

It was the answer to this that Sir Charles had written.

"Here is the photograph," said Lady Bussit, "with your own measurement applied."

She showed it him. A skilfully executed likeness, taken in his baldest time, before his whiskers disappeared.

"And here," she continued, producing a magnificent false head of hair, "is the result."

A loud cry of delight escaped from her husband, as he gently fitted the perruque on his marble-like head.

Lady Bussit whispered in his ear, "You won't mind Robert's beard and mustache now?"

"Not I."

"You will never have another fit."

"I never wish for a better one than this."

So they sat together murmuring in each other's ears.

Then Lady Bussit plucked up courage, and showed him her magnificent chignon.

"Let us be grateful to Heaven," said Sir Charles. That night they rested happily.

Sir Charles rose at dawn. He was for driving over to Tuppennie Bussit in triumph.

Horses, flags, drums, trumpets, and two troops of his own raising, with colors.

4

On their road, Sir Charles, remembering the address to which the she-bear had been carried, drove a little out of his way, and called there.

It was a Barber's shop. Over the door was an announcement to the effect that a large bear had just been slaughtered, and that the grease was invaluable.

Sir Charles's servants returned laden with three dozen pots of the "Capillary Confection." This was the title given to the pomade by the barber, who had invented it himself.

Robert, from the Tower of Teazer, saw the happy pair drive into the village.

Young farmers were out cantering about. Old peasants in their carts. Children on donkeys. Peasants from the plough. All shouting together in their joy at the return of their kind landlord and his loving wife, and unable to restrain their admiration of Sir Charles's glossy locks, flowing beard, and brown mustache.

Before they reached the village four hundred horsemen accompanied the carriage, while at least four hundred more, unaccustomed to the saddle, were on their backs in the dust.

The church-bells rang; everybody cheered; and seventy-five pensioners, whose united ages amounted six thousand seven hundred and fifty years, sang a horus of one hour and a half's duration, by the Church clock, which played the accompaniment.

At this Lady Bussit began to cry: Sir Charles bowed right and left, taking off his wig to the people with great delight and pride. It was a Royal Progress.

Molly Borne, seated on the back seat of the carriage, threw her boots in the air for luck.

A roar of cheers burst from the crowd at that inspired action of a woman whose face and eyes seemed to be on fire. Lady Bussit turned pale, but a skilful movement of her head avoided the second boot. Then they all stood up and shouted.

It was open house that night to every one.

Paupers from the workhouse came into Tuppennie Bussit Hall, and slept wherever they liked, only requesting to have their shoes well polished and bright early, and a cup of chocolate half an hour before they got up in the morning.

Farmers played the piano, and their elders danced in the drawing-room. Others spent the night in the wine-cellars. No man or woman was denied. Oxen were roasted whole in every room in the house, kegs were broached, and ale, cider, port, sherry, and champagne flowed down the stairs in rich, frothy streams. It was open house that night to all as it had been four hundred years ago.

CHAPTER XII.

OBERT BUSSIT was served with a Declaration and a Writ. It was in three counts in their shortest and most simple form :—

1st. That the said Robert Bussit of ——, in the county of ——, on the —— day of ——, in the year of ——, did, of his own malice aforethought, and all to the contrary notwithstanding, molest, annoy, and evict, *vi et armis*, from statutable and possessory rights the plaintiff in this action, and that the aforesaid Robert Bussit did, on the same day as aforesaid, that is, on the —— day of ——, in the year of ——, cause the plaintiff as aforesaid to be seized and removed against his will and consent to a place set apart by law for the legal retention of such Quadrupeds, Bipeds, and others not being *feræ naturæ* or *lusus naturæ*, in the Park of the Regent in the County of Middlesex.

2d. *That the said* Robert Bussit (etc., etc., as before) *did* (much the same as mentioned in the above count) . . . and in consequence of such act or acts done and executed of malice aforethought as aforesaid, the plaintiff, Sir Charles Bussit, of Tupennie Bussit, in the county of ——, on the day of ——, in the year of ——, does claim and cause to be claimed all that part, portion, and inalienable right of *quod ci deforceat*, such right not being barred by the usurpation of the incorporeal hereditament whereof as aforesaid the afore-mentioned Robert, etc., etc.

3d Count. *And that* (all re-stated as above at full length) *the plaintiff thereupon claims £36,000 for damnum et injuria, and hereby on the day of* ——, *etc.*, etc.

Robert Bussit sold his house, pulled down the Tower of Teazer, and paid the money. It was a sickener ; it broke his spirit.

Defeated at every point, Robert fell into a deep dejection, and took to tumbling for a livelihood. He and his wife and child hired themselves out as "Signor Bussittini and Talented family." They practised standing on their heads for hours every day. One thing was clear : they would never again alight on their legs.

His father-in-law once took tickets for his benefit. This was all they had to live upon.

He applied to Mr. Juff for an equestrian **drama.** Mr. Juff wrote it. This crushed him utterly.

He travelled about the country with it for some time ; then he travelled about without it.

Much journeying brought him in contact with all sorts of people, for whom he had but one question, " Do you know my cousin, Lady Bussit ? "

Persons to whom this query was put, thought it was a conundrum, and gave it up.

Then he hated everybody worse than ever.

One day he heard the bells of some church ringing.

" What's that for ? " he asked, sharply.

" Young Bussit," answered the man.

Robert took up a log of wood, and rushed at **him.** " I'll teach you," he cried, " to ring bells."

The man ducked, and ran out.

CHAPTER XIII.

UR story now makes a bold jump.
Everybody is twenty years older.
Sir Charles Bussit has one son:
Robert one daughter.

Robert is once more residing at Bussit, in a small cottage. He hates his cousin worse than ever.

One day Mr. Banjo, now the Perpetual Curate of Tuppennie Bussit, came to Sir Charles to complain.

"There was," he said, " a middle-aged person, in fact a female, preaching in the village; and as she preached better than he did, nobody came to hear *him*."

Sir Charles decided to judge for himself. Being a Magistrate, he was legally entitled to do so.

A large crowd was gathered round the woman, who was perched on a tub.

He recognized her at once—La Dorchester.

She spoke briefly, but forcibly.

She lashed Drunkenness, and then took another subject in hand, Quarrels in families.

"Look here," she exclaimed, "why do you quarrel? Birds in their little nests agree, and 'tis a shameful sight," (*murmurs from the crowd.*) "When children of one family " (*more murmurs*) "fall out, and scratch and fight." ("*So be it!*" *from the crowd.*) "What's that? Watts. Well now, is that true? ("*No!*" *heartily from the crowd.*) "You know better than that." (" *We do!*" *from crowd.*) "Very well, then. If you know better, *do* better." (" *We will, we will!*" *from crowd.*) "Set an example to Sir Charles " ("*Hooray!*" *from crowd.*) "and Robert." ("*Yah!*" *from crowd.*) Teach 'em that their little hands were never made to tear, and bite, and fight? Ask them, How are you *to-morrow?*" ("*Ah!*" *from* Sir Charles *and the crowd.*) "Ask 'em, How they'd like it themselves?" (" *Ah!*" *from* Robert *and the crowd.*) "Oh! my friends, be assured that I'm right, and everybody else is wrong." (" *You are! you are!*") "Why do you beat your carpets? Why give more?" (*Sobs.*) "Many to whom this question is put will reply, I can read, write, but I cannot speak it." ("*Yes, yes!*") "Oh, my Christian friends, the Christy Minstrels *never* perform out of London, and none

other is genuine unless signed with the trade mark."
(*Convulsions in crowd, and several people led away
howling.*)　" What matters it, after all, if we can only
strike on the box? Let us act up to it! More! Let
us double up our perambulators, and moisten the
starch of Glenfield with the soothing syrup of the
maternal Winslow; then while we Bantingize in a
daylight of Ozone, we can indeed aspire to the glorious light of the Ozokerit! !"

The fair orator delivered these words with such
fire, such feeling, such clarion-like eloquence, that
from the people, at first spell-bound, there arose so
loud, so heartfelt a cry of grateful joy as is seldom
heard from the lips of those who are perfectly satisfied with themselves, in their glossy hats and shiny
boots, on Sunday afternoons.

CHAPTER XIV

HE Preacher had vanished. But the fire of her words remained, and moved statues. The Cousins quivered

Then Robert spoke. "Chawles . . . ."

Sir Charles lifted his head loftily, but there was a tear in his right eye, unwiped.

Robert continued, behind his hat, "Chawles . . . . I have been wrong. I am sorry we are enemies. Good·morning."

Then Sir Charles's Boy ran out, and Robert's Daughter rushed into his arms.

Thus the Children's love wore out their father's hate.

*   *   *   *   *   *

La Dorchester meeting Molly Borne in the lane, called upon her to repent.

" Never ! " answered Molly.

And she never did; not having, as she said, anything to repent of.

* * * * * *

Robert Bussit one evening said to Sniffkin, "Old boy, never hate anybody."

Sniffkin bowed coldly. He didn't like being called "old boy," and never spoke to Robert again.

* * * * * *

Sir Charles and Lady Bussit lead a peaceful life. They both wear their own hair now, and it is quite gray.

Their son and his wife often come to dinner, and have excellent appetites. After the meal, Juff, who has made the house one of his homes, reads them his plays, and sings little compositions of his own to them, playing on the mandoline. In consequence, they go to bed early.

* * * * * *

You, Gentlemen and Ladies, who read this, be firm, and if you've done anything wrong, don't be misled by this novel into doing it again.

Be kind, be generous, buy Juff's books, and read Juff's writings.

When in doubt, ask Juff.

Never consult a Solicitor,—go to Juff.

My experience is, that we're, all of us, generally very nice sort of people, except the nasty ones.

So let us end with a couplet of one of England's greatest writers:

"Where is the man of truest stuff—
The Best, the Greatest . . It is JUFF."

APPENDIX.

From the Editor* to the Author of " A Treble Temptation."

MY DEAR OLD JUFFY,—*Your Novel is excellent. Of course I congratulate you upon its admirable finish. Permit me to ask you, in consequence of various inquiries on the subject, addressed to me in my editorial capacity, why is it called " A Treble Temptation ? "*

I remain, my dear old Juffy, yours most Affectionately,
THE EDITOR.

From MR. J., *Author of &c., &c., to the Editor of P.*

DEAR SIR,—*May not a father christen his own child as he will ? I choose to call this Novel " A Treble Temptation." Don't call me " Old Juffy."*
Yours, decidedly.

---

* The Editor of *P-nch*, to which journal, as has been already stated in this novel, Mr. Juff was a constant contributor. The *Treble Temptation* first appeared in *P-nch*.

From the Editor to MR J.

MY DEAR JUFF,—*I do not dispute your right to christen your own charming Novel. But how does the title apply?*

I remain, yours, dear Juff, affectionately,
THE EDITOR.

From MR. J. *to the Editor.*

SIR—*I can't be Œdipus and Sphinx. It is a Treble Temptation, and the best Novel I've ever done.*

Yours,

J.

From the Editor to MR. J.

DEAR MR. JUFF—*You are perfectly at liberty to hold your own opinion as to the merits of the Novel in question. I shall not discuss that point with you. I confess I do not see what the temptation was, or why it was treble. Permit me to add that I am not alone in my failure of perception.*

I remain, Sir, yours sincerely,
THE EDITOR.

From Mr. J. *to the Editor.*

Sir—Quod scripsi scripsi. *What I have scribbled I have scribbled. I am answerable to no man. Certainly not to* you. *You have been a dramatic author, and probably are acquainted with French. If so, mark my reply to your question, " Pêche et Cherche !*

J.

From the Editor of P. to Mr. J.

Sir—*You are, I regret to say, begging the question, while I am begging the answer. The point at issue between yourself and the public, which I now editorially represent, is the exact application of the title, " Treble Temptation," bestowed by you upon your Novel, Tale, or whatever the work may be* out *of your own estimation. Oblige me with a satisfactory answer. Should you fail to comply with my request, I shall certainly publish the correspondence.*

Yours, &c., &c.

From Mr. J. *to the Editor.*

Publish what you like. The name of the Novel is " The Treble Temptation."

J.

5

[The Editor owes it to himself and the public, to inform them that, after some search, he has discovered that the *trebleness* of the Temptation must be looked for in the three reasons for Robert's hatred of his cousin Charles. These will be found in the First Chapter. Our readers may perhaps have formed some other conclusion ; but at all events they will agree with the one at which Mr. Juff has arrived, namely, the conclusion of his novel. And here let the Editor explain, that, in his first letter to he author, he congratulated him " upon its admira-)le finish." This expression might be taken as ap-)licable to the style : it is *not* to be so taken.—ED. *P.*]

F. C. BURNAND.

GEORGE DE BARNWELL.

By Sir E. L. B. L., Bart

VOL. I.

 N the Morning of Life the Truthful wooed the Beautiful, and their offspring was Love. Like his Divine parents, He is eternal. He has his Mother's ravishing smile; his Father's steadfast eyes. He rises every day, fresh and glorious as the untired Sun-God. He is Eros, the ever young. Dark, dark were this world of ours had either Divinity left it—dark without the day-beams of the Latonian Charioteer, darker yet without the dædal Smile of the God of the Other Bow! Dost know him, reader?

Old is he, Eros, the ever young. He and Time were children together. Chronos shall die, too; but Love is imperishable. Brightest of the Divinities, where hast thou not been sung? Other worships pass away ; the idols for whom pyramids were raised lie in the desert crumbling and almost nameless , the Olympians are fled, their fanes' no longer rise among the quivering olive-groves of Ilissus, or crown the emerald-islets of the amethyst Ægean ! These are gone, but thou remainest. There is still a garland for thy temple, a heifer for thy stone. A heifer? Ah, many a darker sacrifice. Other blood is shed at thy altars, Remorseless One, and the Poet Priest who ministers at thy Shrine draws his auguries from the bleeding hearts of men ! .

While Love hath no end, can the Bard ever cease singing ? In Kingly and Heroic ages, 'twas of Kings and Heroes that the Poet spake. · But in these, our times, the Artisan hath his voice as well as the Monarch. The people To-day is King, and we chronicle his woes, as They of old did the sacrifice of the princely Iphigenia, or the fate of the crowned Agamemnon.

Is Odysseus less august in his rags than in his purple ? Fate, Passion, Mystery, the Victim, the Avenger, the Hate that harms, the Furies that tear, the Love that bleeds, are not these with us Still ? are not these still the weapons of the Artist? the colors of his palette ? the chords of his lyre ? Listen !

I tell thee a tale—not of Kings—but of Men—not
of Thrones, but of Love, and Grief, and ·Crime.
Listen, and but once more. 'Tis for the last time
(probably) these fingers shall sweep the strings.

E. L. B. L.

NOONDAY IN CHEPE.

'Twas noonday in Chepe. High Tide in the
mighty River City!—its banks well-nigh overflowing
with the myriad-waved Stream of Man! The top-
pling wains, bearing the produce of a thousand marts ;
the gilded equipage of the Millionary ; the humbler,
but yet larger vehicle from the green metropolitan sub-
urbs (the Hanging Gardens of our Babylon), in which
every traveller might, for a modest remuneration,
take a republican seat ; the mercenary caroche, with
its private freight ; the brisk curricle of the letter-
carrier, robed in royal scarlet : these and a thousand
others were laboring and pressing onward, and locked
and bound and hustling together in the narrow channel of Chepe. The imprecations of the charioteers
were terrible. From the noble's broidered hammer-
cloth, or the driving-seat of the common coach, each
driver assailed the other with floods of ribald satire
The pavid matron with the one vehicle (speeding to

the Bank for her semestrial pittance) shrieked and trembled ; the angry Dives hastening to his office (to add another thousand to his heap), thrust his head over the blazoned panels, and displayed an eloquence of objurgation which his very Menials could not equal ; the dauntless street urchins, as they gayly threaded the Labyrinth of Life, enjoyed the perplexities and quarrels of the scene, and exacerbated the already furious combatants by their poignant infantile satire. And the Philosopher, as he regarded the hot strife and struggle of these Candidates in the race for Gold, thought with a sigh of the Truthful and the Beautiful, and walked on melancholy and serene.

'Twas noon in Chepe. The warerooms were thronged. The flaunting windows of the mercers attracted many a purchaser : the glittering panes behind which Birmingham had glazed its simulated silver, induced rustics to pause : although only noon, the savory odors of the Cook Shops tempted the over-hungry citizen to the bun of Bath, or to the flagrant pottage that mocks the turtle's flavor—the turtle ! *O dapibus supremi grata testudo Jovis !* I am an Alderman when I think of thee ! Well : it was noon in Chepe.

But were all battling for gain there? Among the many brilliant shops whose casements shone upon Chepe, there stood one a century back (about which period our tale opens) devoted to the sale of Colonial produce. A rudely carved image of a negro, with a fantastic plume and apron of variegated feathers, decorated the lintel. The East and West had sent their contributions to replenish the window.

The poor slave had toiled, died perhaps, to produce yon pyramid of swarthy sugar marked "ONLY 6½*d.*"—That catty box, on which was the epigraph "STRONG FAMILY CONGO ONLY 3*s.* 9*d.*," was from the country of Confutzee—that heap of dark produce bore the legend "TRY OUR REAL NUT"—'Twas Cocoa—and that nut the Cocoa-nut, whose milk has refreshed the traveller and perplexed the natural philosopher. The shop in question was, in a word, a Grocer's.

In the midst of the shop and its gorgeous contents sat one, who, to judge from his appearance (though 'twas a difficult task, as, in sooth, his back was turned), had just reached that happy period of life when the Boy is expanding into the Man. O Youth, Youth! Happy and Beautiful! O fresh and roseate dawn of life; when the dew yet lies on the flowers, ere they have been scorched and withered by Passion's fiery Sun ! Immersed in thought or study, and indifferent to the din around him, sat the boy. A careless guardian was he of the treasures confided to him. The crowd passed in Chepe ; he never marked it. The sun shone on Chepe ; he only asked that it should illumine the page he read. The knave might filch his treasures ; he was heedless of the knave. The customer might enter ; but his book was all in all to him.

And indeed a customer *was* there ; a little hand was tapping on the counter with a pretty impatience ; a pair of arch eyes were gazing at the boy, admiring, perhaps, his manly proportions through the homely and tightened garments he wore.

" Ahem ! sir ! I say young man ! " the customer exclaimed.

" *Ton d'apameibomenos prosephe,*" read on the student, his voice choked with emotion. " What language ! " he said ; " how rich, how noble, how sonorous ! *prosephe podas* "—

The customer burst out in a fit of laughter so shrill and cheery, that the young Student could not but turn round, and blushing, for the first time remarked her, "A pretty grocer's boy you are," she cried, "with your applepiebomenos and your French and lingo. Am I to be kept waiting for hever!"

"Pardon, fair Maiden," said with high-bred courtesy; "'twas not French I read, 'twas the Godlike language of the blind old bard. In what can I be serviceable to ye, lady?" and to spring from his desk, to smooth his apron, to stand before her the obedient Shop Boy, the Poet no more, was the work of a moment.

"I might haved prigged this box of figs," the damsel said good-naturedly, "and you'd never turned round."

"They came from the country of Hector," the boy said. "Would you have currants, lady? These once bloomed in the island gardens of the blue Ægean. They are uncommon fine ones, and the figure is low; they're fourpence-halfpenny a pound. Would ye mayhap make trial of our teas? We do not advertise, as some folks do: but sell as low as any other house."

"You're precious young to have all these good things," the girl exclaimed, not unwilling, seemingly, to prolong the conversation. "If I was you, and stood behind the counter, I should be eating figs the whole day long."

" Time was," answered the lad, "and not long since, I thought so too. I thought I never should be tired of figs. But my old uncle bade me take my fill, and now in sooth I am aweary of them."

" I think you gentlemen are always so," the coquette said.

" Nay, say not so, fair stranger!" the youth replied, his face kindling as he spoke, and his eagle eyes flashing fire. " Figs' pall; but oh! the Beautiful never does. Figs rot; but oh! the truthful is Eternal. I was born, lady, to grapple with the Lofty and the Ideal. My soul yearns for the Visionary. I stand behind the counter, it is true; but I ponder here upon the deeds of heroes, and muse over the thoughts of sages. What is grocery for one who has ambition? What sweetness has Muscovado to him who hath tasted of Poesy? The Ideal, lady, I often think, is the true Real, and the Actual but a visionary hallucination. But pardon me; with what may I serve thee? "

" I came only for sixpenn'orth of tea-dust," the girl said, with a faltering voice ; " but oh, I should like to hear you speak on forever ! "

Only for sixpenn'orth of tea-dust? Girl, thou camest for other things! Thou lovedst his voice?

Siren! what was the witchery of thine own? **He** deftly made up the packet, and placed it in the little hand. She paid for her small purchase, and with a farewell glance of her lustrous eyes, she left him. She passed slowly through the portals, and in a moment more was lost in the crowd. It was **noon** in Chepe. And George de Barnwell was alone.

E have selected the following episodical chapter in preference to anything relating to the mere story of George de Barnwell, with which most readers are familiar.

Up to this passage (extracted from the beginning of Vol. II.) the tale is briefly thus :

The rogue of a Millwood has come back every day to the grocer's shop in Chepe, wanting some sugar or some nutmeg, or some figs, half a dozen times in the week.

She and George de Barnwell have vowed to each other an eternal attachment.

This flame acts violently upon George. His bosom swells with ambition. His genius breaks out prodigiously. He talks about the Good, the Beautiful, the Ideal, etc., in and out of all season, and is virtuous and eloquent almost beyond belief—in fact like Devereux or P. Clifford, or E. Aram, Esquires.

Inspired by Millwood and love, George robs the
till, and mingles in the world which he is destined to
ornament. He outdoes all the dandies, all the wits, all
the scholars, and all the voluptuaries of the age—an
definite period of time between Queen Anne and
George II.—dines with Curll at St. John's Gate,
pinks Colonel Charteris in a duel behind Montague
House, is initiated into the intrigues of the Cheva-
lier St. George, whom he entertains at his sumptuous
pavilion at Hampstead, and likewise in disguise at
the shop in Cheapside.

His uncle, the owner of the shop, a surly curmud-
geon with very little taste for the True and Beautiful, has retired from business to the pastoral village
in Cambridgeshire from which the noble Barnwell
came. George's cousin Annabel is, of course, con-
sumed with a secret passion for him.

Some trifling inaccuracies · may be remarked in
the ensuing brilliant little chapter; but it must be
remembered that the author wished to present an
age at a glance : and the dialogue is quite as fine
and correct as that in the " Last of the Barons," or
in " Eugene Aram," or other works of our author, in
which Sentiment and History, or the True and Beautiful, are united.

CHAPTER XXIV.

THOSE who frequent the dismal and enormous Mansions of Silence which society has raised to Ennui in that Omphalos of town, Pall Mall, and which, because they knock you down with their dulness, are called Clubs no doubt ; those who yawn from a bay-window in St. James's Street, at a half-score of other dandies gasping from another bay-window over the way ; those who consult a dreary evening paper for news, or satisfy themselves with the jokes of the miserable " Punch " by way of wit ; the men about town of the present day, in a word, can have but little idea of London some six or eight score years back. Thou pudding-sided old dandy of St. James's Street, with thy lacquered boots, thy dyed whiskers, and thy suffocating waistband, what art thou to thy brilliant predecessor in the same quarter ? The Brougham from which thou descend-

est at the portal of the " Carlton " or the " Travel
ler's," is like everybody else's ; thy black coat has no
more plaits, nor buttons, nor fancy in it than thy
neighbor's ; thy hat was made on the very block
on which Lord Addlepate's was cast, who has just
entered the Club before thee. You and he yawn together out of the same omnibus-box every night ;
you fancy yourselves men of pleasure ; you fancy
yourselves men of fashion ; you fancy yourselves
men of taste ; in fancy, in taste, in opinion, in philosophy, the newspaper legislates for you ; it is there
you get your jokes and your thoughts, and your facts
and your wisdom—poor Pall Mall dullards. Stupid
slaves of the press, on the ground which you at present occupy, there were men of wit and pleasure and
fashion, some five and twenty lustres ago.

We are at Button's—the well-known sign of the
" Turk's Head." The crowd of periwigged heads at
the windows—the swearing chairmen round the steps
(the blazoned and coronalled panels of whose ve-
hicles denote the lofty rank of their owners),—the
thong of embroidered beaux entering or departing,
and rendering the air fragrant with the odors of
pulvillio and pomander, proclaim the celebrated
resort of London's Wit and Fashion. It is the cor-

ner of Regent Street. Carlton House has not yet
been taken down.

A stately gentleman in crimson velvet and gold is
sipping chocolate at one of the tables, in earnest
converse with a friend whose suit is likewise embroidered, but stained by time, or wine mayhap, or
wear. A little deformed gentleman in iron-gray is
reading *The Morning Chronicle* newspaper by the
fire, while a divine, with a broad brogue and a shovel
hat and cassock, is talking freely with a gentleman,
whose star and ribbon, as well as the unmistakable
beauty of his Phidian countenance, proclaim him to
be a member of Britain's aristocracy.

Two ragged youths, the one tall, gaunt, clumsy,
and scrofulous, the other with a wild, careless,
beautiful look, evidently indicating Race, are gazing in at the window, not merely at the crowd in
the celebrated Club, but at Timothy the waiter,
who is removing a plate of that exquisite dish, the
muffin (then newly invented), at the desire of some
of the revellers within.

"I would, Sam," said the wild youth to his companion, "that I had some of my mother Maccles-
field's gold, to enable us to eat of those cates and
mingle with yon springalds and beaux."

" To vaunt a knowledge of the stoical philosophy," said the youth addressed as Sam, " might elicit a smile of incredulity upon the cheek of the parasite of pleasure ; but there are moments in life when History fortifies endurance ; and past study renders present deprivation more bearable. If our pecuniary resources be exiguous, let our resolution, Dick, supply the deficiencies of Fortune. The muffin we desire to-day would little benefit us to-morrow. Poor and hungry as we are, are we less happy, Dick, than yon listless voluptuary who banquets on the food which you covet? "

And the two lads turned away up Waterloo Place, and past the " Parthenon " Club-house, and disappeared to take a meal of cow-heel at a neighboring rook's shop. Their names were Samuel Johnson and Richard Savage.

Meanwhile the conversation at Button's was fast and brilliant. " By Wood's thirteens, and the divvle go wid 'em," cried the Church dignitary in the cassock, "is it in blue and goold ye are this morning, Sir Richard, when you ought to be in seebles? "

" Who's dead, Dean? " said the nobleman, the dean's companion.

" Faix mee Lard Bolingbroke, as sure as mee

6

name's Jonathan Swift — and I'm not so sure of
that neither, for who knows his father's name? —
there's been a mighty cruel murther committed
entirely. A child of Dick Steele's has been bar-
barously slain, dthrawn, and quarthered, and it's
Joe Addison yondther has done it. Ye should
have killed one of your own, Joe, ye thief of the
world."

"I!" said the amazed and Right Honorable
Joseph Addison; "I kill Dick's child! I was god-
father to the last."

"And promised a cup and never sent it," Dick
ejaculated. Joseph looked grave.

"The child I mean is Sir Roger de Coverley,
Knight and Baronet. What made ye kill him, ye
savage Mohock? The whole town is in tears about
the good knight; all the ladies at Church this
afternoon were in mourning; all the booksellers are
wild; and Lintot says not a third of the copies of
'The Spectator' are sold since the death of the
brave old gentleman. And the Dean of St. Patrick's
pulled out "The Spectator" newspaper, containing
the well-known passage regarding Sir Roger's death.
"I bought it but now in 'Wellington Street,'" he said;
"the newsboys were howling all down the Strand."

"What a miracle is Genius—Genius, the Divine
and Beautiful," said a gentleman leaning against the
same fire-place with the deformed cavalier in iron-
gray, and addressing that individual, who was in
fact Mr. Alexander Pope. "What a marvellous gift
is this, and royal privilege of Art! To make the
Ideal more credible than the Actual : to enchain
our hearts, to command our hopes, our regrets, our
tears, for a mere brain-born Emanation : to invest
with life the Incorporeal, and to glamour the cloudy
into substance,—these are the lofty privileges of
the Poet, if I have read poesy aright ; and I am as
familiar with the sounds that rang from Homer's
lyre, as with the strains which celebrate the loss of
Belinda's lovely locks "—(Mr. Pope blushed and
bowed highly delighted) — "these, I say, are the
privileges of the Poet—the Poietes—the Maker—
he moves the world, and asks no lever ; if he cannot
charm death into life, as Orpheus feigned to do, he
can create Beauty out of Nought, and defy Death
by rendering Thought Eternal. Ho! Jemmy, another flask of Nantz."

And the boy — for he who addressed the most
brilliant company of wits in Europe was little more
—emptied the contents of the brandy-flask into a

silver flagon, and quaffed it gayly to the health of the company assembled. 'Twas the third he had taken during the sitting. Presently, and with a graceful salute to the Society, he quitted the coffee-house, and was seen cantering on a magnificent Arab past the National Gallery.

"Who is yon spark in blue and silver? He beats Joe Addison himself, in drinking, and pious Joe is the greatest toper in the three kingdoms," Dick Steele said, good-naturedly.

"His paper in the 'Spectator' beats thy best, Dick, thou sluggard," the Right Honorable Mr. Addison exclaimed. "He is the author of that famous No. 996, for which you have all been giving me the credit."

"The rascal foiled me at capping verses," Dean Swift said, "and won a tenpenny piece of me, plague take him!"

"He has suggested an emendation in my 'Homer,' which proves him a delicate scholar," Mr. Pope exclaimed.

"He knows more of the French king than any man I ever met with; and we must have an eye upon him," said Lord Bolingbroke, then Secretary of State for Foreign Affairs, and, beckoning a suspicious-looking person who was drinking at a side-table, whispered to him something.

Meantime, who was he? where was he, this youth who had struck all the wits of London with admiration? His galloping charger had returned to the City; his splendid court-suit was doffed for the citizen's gaberdine and grocer's humble apron.

George de Barnwell was in Chepe—in Chepe, at the feet of Martha Millwood.

VOL. III.

THE CONDEMNED CELL.

*UID me mollibus implicas lacertis*, my Ellinor? Nay," George added a faint smile illumining his wan but noble features, "why speak to thee in the accents of the Roman poet, which thou comprehendest not? Bright One, there be other things in Life, in Nature, this Inscrutable Labyrinth, this Heart on which thou leanest, which are equally unintelligible to thee! Yes, my pretty one, what is the Unintelligible but the Ideal? what is the Ideal but the Beautiful? what the Beautiful but the Eternal? And the Spirit of Man that would commune with these is like Him who wanders by the *thin poluphloiboio thalasses*, and shrinks awe-struck before that Azure Mystery."

Emily's eyes filled with fresh-gushing dew. "Speak on, speak ever thus, my George," she exclaimed. Barnwell's chains rattled as the confiding girl clung to him. Even Snoggin, the Turnkey appointed to sit with the prisoner, was affected by his noble and appropriate language, and also burst into tears.

"You weep, my Snoggin," the Boy said; "and why? Hath Life been so charming to me that I should wish to retain it? Hath Pleasure no after-Weariness? Ambition no Deception; Wealth no Care; and Glory no Mockery? Psha! I am sick of Success, palled of Pleasure, weary of Wine and Wit, and—nay, start not, my Adelaide—and Woman. I fling away all these things as the Toys of Boyhood. Life is the Soul's Nursery. I am a man, and pine for the Illimitable! Mark you me! Has the Morrow any terrors for me, think ye? Did Socrates falter at his poison? Did Seneca blench in his bath? Did Brutus shirk the sword when his great stake was lost? Did even weak Cleopatra shrink from the Serpent's fatal nip. And why should I? My great Hazard hath been played, and I pay my forfeit. Lie sheathed in my heart, thou flashing Blade! Welcome to my Bosom, thou faithful Serpent; I hug thee, peace-bearing Image of the Eternal? Ha, the hemlock cup! Fill high, boy, for my soul is thirsty for the Infinite! Get ready the bath, friends; prepare me for the feast To-morrow—bathe my limbs in odors, and put ointment in my hair."

"Has for a bath," Snoggin interposed, "they'r not to be 'ad in this ward of the prison ; but I dussay Hemmy will get you a little hoil for your 'air."

The Prisoned One laughed loud and merrily. " My guardian understands me not, pretty one—and thou ? what sayest thou ? From those dear lips me-thinks — *plura sunt oscula quam sententiæ*—I kiss away thy tears, dove !—they will flow apace when I am gone, then they will dry, and presently these fair eyes will shine on another, as they have beamed on poor George Barnwell. Yet wilt thou not all forget him, sweet one. He was an honest fellow, and had a kindly heart for all the world said "—

" That, that he had," cried the jailer and the girl in voices gurgling with emotion. And you who read ! you unconvicted Convict — you murderer, though haply you have slain no one—you Felon *in posse* if not *in esse*—deal gently with one who has used the Opportunity that has failed thee—and be-lieve that the Truthful and the Beautiful bloom sometimes in the dock and the convict's tawny Gaber-dine !

*　*　*　*　*　*　*　*　*　*

In the matter for which he suffered, George could

never be brought to acknowledge that he was at all in the wrong. " It may be an error of judgment," he said to the Venerable Chaplain of the jail, " but it is no crime. Were it Crime, I should feel Remorse. Where there is no remorse, Crime cannot exist. I am not sorry: therefore, I am innocent. Is the proposition a fair one?

The excellent Doctor admitted that it was not to be contested.

" And wherefore, sir, should I have sorrow," the Boy resumed, "for ridding the world of a sordid worm ; * of a man whose very soul was dross, and who never had a feeling for the Truthful and the Beautiful? When I stood before my uncle in the moonlight, in the gardens of the ancestral halls of the De Barnwells, I felt that it was the Nemesis come to overthrow him. 'Dog,' I said to the trembling slave, 'tell me where thy Gold is. *Thou* hast no

---

* This is a gross plagiarism : the above sentiment is expressed much more eloquently in the ingenious romance of " Eugene Aram : "— " The burning desires I have known—the resplendent visions I have nursed—the sublime aspirings that have lifted me so often from sense and clay : these tell me, that whether for good or ill, I am the thing of an immortality, and the creature of a God. . . . I have destroyed a man noxious to the world ! with the wealth by which he afflicted society, I have been the means of blessing many."

use for it.   I can spend it in relieving the Poverty
on which thou tramplest ; aiding Science, which
thou knowest not ; in uplifting Art, to which thou
art blind.   Give Gold, and thou art free.'   But he
spake not, and I slew him."

"I would not have this doctrine vulgarly promul-
gated," said the admirable chaplain, "for its general
practice might chance to do harm.   Thou, my son,
the Refined, the Gentle, the Loving and Beloved,
the Poet and Sage, urged by what I cannot but think
a grievous error, hast appeared as Avenger.   Think
what would be the world's condition, were men without any Yearning after the Ideal to attempt to re-
organize Society, to redistribute Property, to avenge
Wrong."

"A rabble of pygmies scaling Heaven," said the
noble though misguided young Prisoner.   "Prome-
theus was a Giant, and he fell."

"Yes, indeed, my brave youth !" the benevolent
Dr. Fuzwig exclaimed, clasping the Prisoner's marble and manacled hand ; "and the Tragedy of To-
morrow will teach the World that Homicide is not to
be permitted even to the most amiable Genius, and
that the lover of the Ideal and the Beautiful, as thou
art, my son, must respect the Real likewise."

" Look ! here is supper ! " cried Barnwell gayly. " This is the Real, Doctor ; let us respect it and fall to." He partook of the meal as joyously as if it had been one of his early festals ; but the worthy chaplain could scarcely eat it for tears.

WILLIAM M. THACKERAY.

A PROPHETIC ACCOUNT OF A GRAND NATURAL EPIC POEM, TO BE ENTITLED "THE WELLINGTONIAD," AND TO BE PUBLISHED a.d. 2824. (November, 1824.)

HOW I became a prophet it is not very important to the reader to know. Nevertheless I feel all the anxiety which, under similar circumstances, troubled the sensitive mind of Sidrophel ; and, like him, am eager to vindicate myself from the suspicion of having practiced forbidden arts, or held intercourse with beings of another world. I solemnly declare, therefore, that I never saw a ghost, like Lord Lyttleton ; consulted a gipsy, like Josephine ; or heard my name pronounced by an absent person, like Dr. Johnson. Though it is now almost as usual for gentlemen to appear at the moment of their death to their friends as to call on them during their life, none of my acquaintance have been so polite as to pay me that customary attention I have derived my knowledge neither from the dea~ nor from the living ; neither from the lines of a hand, nor from the grounds of a tea-cup ; neither from the stars of the firmament, nor from the fiends of the abyss. I have never, like the Wesley family, heard "that mighty leading angel," who " drew after him the third part of heaven's sons," scratching in my cupboard.   I have never been enticed to sign any of those delusive bonds which have been the ruin of so many poor creatures ; and, having always been an indifferent horseman, I have been careful not to venture myself on a broomstick.

My insight into futurity, like that of George Fox the Quaker, and that of our great and philosophic poet, Lord Byron, is derived from simple presentiment. This is a far less artificial process than those which are employed by some others.   Yet my prediction will, I believe, be found more correct then theirs, or at all events, as Sir Benjamin Backbite says in the play, " more circumstantial."

I prophesy then, that in the year 2824, according to our present reckoning, a grand national Epic Poem, worthy to be compared with the Iliad, the Æneid, or the Jerusalem, will be published in London.

Men naturally take an interest in the adventures of every eminent writer.   I will, therefore, gratify the laudable curiosity, which, on this occasion, will

doubtless be universal, by prefixing to my account of
the poem a concise memoir of the poet.

Richard Quongti will be born at Westminster on
the 1st of July, 2786. He will be the younger son
of the younger branch of one of the most respectable
families in England. He will be lineally descended
from Quongti, the famous Chinese liberal, who, after
the failure of the heroic attempt of his party to ob
tain a constitution from the Emperor Fim Fam, will
take refuge in England, in the twenty-third century.
Here his descendants will obtain considerable note;
and one branch of the family will be raised to the
peerage.

Richard, however, though destined to exalt his
family to distinction far nobler than any which wealth
or titles can bestow, will be born to a very scanty
fortune. He will display in his early youth such
striking talents as will attract the notice of Viscount
Quongti. his third cousin, then secretary of state for
the Steam Department. At the expense of this eminent nobleman, he will be sent to prosecute his
studies at the university of Timbuctoo. To that
illustrious seat of muses all the ingenuous of youth of
every country will then be attracted by the high
scientific character of Professor Quashaboo, and the

eminent literary attainments of Professor Kissey Kicky. In spite of this formidable competition, however, Quongti will acquire the highest honors in every department of knowledge, and will obtain the esteem of his associates by his amiable and unaffected manners. The guardians of the young Duke of Carrington, premier peer of England, and the last remaining scion of the ancient and illustrious house of Smith, will be desirous to secure so able an instructor for their ward. With the Duke, Quongti will perform the grand tour, and visit the polished courts of Sydney and Capetown. After prevailing on his pupil, with great difficulty, to subdue a violent and imprudent passion which he had conceived for a Hottentot lady, of great beauty and accomplishments indeed, but of dubious character, he will travel with him to the United States of America. But that tremendous war which will be fatal to American liberty will, at that time, be raging through the whole federation. At New York the travellers will hear of the final defeat and death of the illustrious champion of freedom, Jonathan Higginbottom, and of the elevation of Ebenezer Hogsflesh to the perpetual Presidency. They will not chose to proceed in a journey which would expose them to the insults of that brutal soldiery, whose cruelty and rapacity will have devastated Mexico and Columbia, and now, at length, enslaved their own country.

On their return to England, A. D. 2810, the death of the Duke will compel his preceptor to seek for a subsistence by literary labors. His fame will be raised by many small productions of considerable merit ; and he will at last obtain a permanent place in the highest class of writers by his great epic poem.

The celebrated work will become, with unexampled rapidity, a popular favorite. The sale will be so beneficial to the author that, instead of going about the dirty streets on his velocipede, he will be enabled to set up his balloon.

The character of this noble poem will be so finely and justly given in the Timbuctoo Review for April, 2825, that I cannot refrain from translating the passage. The author will be our poet's old preceptor, Professor Kissey Kickey.

"In pathos, in splendor of language, in sweetness of versification, Mr. Quongti has long been considered as unrivalled. In his exquisite poem on the *Ornithorhynchus Paradoxus* all these qualities are displayed in their greatest perfection. How exquis-

itely does that work arrest and embody the undefined
and vague shadows which flit over an imaginative
mind. The cold worlding may not comprehend it;
but it will find a response in the bosom of every
youthful poet, of every enthusiastic lover, who has
seen an *Ornithorhynchus Paradoxus* by moonlight.
But we were yet to learn that he possessed the com-
prehension, the judgment, and the fertility of mind
indispensable to the epic poet.

"It is difficult to conceive a plot more perfect
than that of the 'Wellingtoniad.' It is most faithful
to the manners of the age to which it relates. It
preserves exactly all the historical circumstances,
and interweaves them most artfully with all the
speciosa miracla of supernatural agency."

Thus far the learned Professor of Humanity in the
university of Timbuctoo. I fear that the critics of
our time will form an opinion diametrically opposite
as to these very points. Some will, I fear, be dis-
gusted by the machinery, which is derived from the
mythology of ancient Greece. I can only say that,
in the twenty-ninth century, that machinery will be
universally in use among poets; and that Quongti
will use it, partly in conformity with the general
practice, and partly from a veneration, perhaps ex-

7

cessive, for the great remains of classical antiquity, which will then, as now, be assiduously read by every man of education ; though Tom Moore's songs will be forgotten, and only three copies of Lord Byron's works will exist : one in the possession of King George the Nineteenth, one in the Duke of Carrington's collection, and one in the library of the British Museum. Finally, should any good people be concerned to hear that Pagan fictions will so long retain their influence over literature, let them reflect that, as the Bishop of St. David's says, in his " Proofs of the Inspiration of the Sibylline Verses," read at the last meeting of the Royal Society of Literature, " at all events, a Pagan is not a Papist."

Some readers of the present day may think that Quongti is by no means entitled to the compliments which his Negro critic pays him on his adherence to the historical circumstances of the time in which he has chosen his subject : that, where he introduces any trait of our manners, it is in the wrong place, and that he confounds the customs of our age with those of much more remote periods. I can only say that the charge is infinitely more applicable to Homer, Virgil and Tasso. If, therefore, the reader should detect, in the following abstract of the plot, any little deviation

from strict historical accuracy, let him reflect, for a
moment, whether Agamemnon would not have found
as much to censure in the Iliad,—Dido in the Æneid,
—or Godfrey in the Jerusalem. Let him not suffer
his opinions to depend on circumstances which cannot
possibly affect the truth or falsehood of the represen-
tation. If it be possible for a single man to kill hun-
dreds in battle, the impossibility is not diminished
by distance of time. If it be as certain that Rinaldo
never disenchanted a forest in Palestine as it is that
the Duke of Wellington never disenchanted the forest
of Soignies, can we, as rational men, tolerate the one
story and ridicule the other? Of this, at least, I am
certain, that whatever excuse we have for admiring
the plots of those famous poems, our children will
have for extolling that of the " Wellingtoniad."

I shall proceed to give a sketch of the narrative.
The subject is " The Reign of the Hundred Days."

BOOK I. The poem commences, in form, with a
solemn proposition of the subject. Then the muse
is invoked to give the poet accurate information as
to the cause of so terrible a commotion. The answer
to this question, being, it is to be supposed, the joint
production of the poet and the muse, ascribes the
event to circumstances which have hitherto eluded

all the research of political writers, namely, the influence of the god Mars, who, we are told, had some forty years before usurped the conjugal rights of old Carlo Buonaparte, and given birth to Napoleon. By his incitement it was that the emperor with his devoted companions was now on the sea, returning to his ancient dominions. The gods were at present, fortunately for the adventurer, feasting with the Ethiopians, whose entertainments, according to the ancient custom described by Homer, they annually attended, with the same sort of condescending gluttony which now carries the cabinet to Guildhall on the 9th of November. Neptune was, in consequence, absent, and unable to prevent the enemy of his favorite island from crossing his element. Boreas, however, who had his abode on the banks of the Russian ocean, and who, like Thetis in the Iliad, was not of sufficient quality to have an invitation to Ethiopia, resolves to destroy the armament which brings war and danger to his beloved Alexander. He accordingly raises a storm which is most powerfully described. Napoleon bewails the inglorious fate for which he seems to be reserved. "Oh! thrice happy," says he, "those who were frozen to death at Krasnoi, or slaughtered at Leipsic. Oh,

Kutusoff, bravest of the Russians, wherefore was I not permitted to fall by thy victorious sword ?" He then offers a prayer to Æolus, and vows to him a sacrifice of a black ram. In consequence, the god recalls his turbulent subject ; the sea is calmed ; and the ship anchors in the port of Frejus. Napoleon and Bertrand, who is always called the faithful Bertrand, land to explore the country ; Mars meets them disguised as a lancer of the guard, wearing the cross of the Legion of Honor. He advises them to apply for necessaries of all kinds to the governor, shows them the way, and disappears with a strong smell of gunpowder. Napoleon makes a pathetic speech, and enters the governor's house. Here he sees hanging up a fine print of the battle of Auster-litz, himself in the foreground giving his orders. This puts him in high spirits ; he advances and salutes the governor, who receives him most loyally, gives him an entertainment, and, according to the usage of all epic hosts, insists after dinner on a full narration of all that has happened to him since the battle of Leipsic.

BOOK II. Napoleon carries his narrative from the battle of Leipsic to his abdication. But, as we shall have a great quantity of fighting on our hands, I think it best to omit the details.

Book III. Napoleon describes his sojourn at Elba and his return ; how he was driven by stress of weather to Sardinia, and fought with the harpies there ; how he was then carried southward to Sicily, where he generously took on board an English sailor, whom a man-of-war had unhappily left there, and who was in imminent danger of being devoured by the Cyclops ; how he landed in the bay of Naples, saw the Sibyl, and descended to Tartarus ; how he held a long and pathetic conversation with Poniatowski whom he found wandering unburied on the banks of the Styx ; how he swore to give him a splendid funeral ; how he had also an affectionate interview with Desaix ; how Moreau and Sir Ralph Abercrombie fled at the sight of him. He relates that he then re-embarked, and met with nothing of importance till the commencement of the storm with which the poem opens.

Book IV. The scene changes to Paris. Fame, in the garb of an express, brings intelligence of the landing of Napoleon. The king performs a sacrifice : but the entrails are unfavorable ; and the victim is without a heart. He prepares to encounter the invader. A young captain of the guard,—the son of Maria Antoinette by Apollo,—in the shape of a fiddler,

rushes in to tell him that Napoleon is approaching
with a vast army. The royal forces are drawn out
for battle. Full catalogues are given of the regiments
on both sides: their colonels, lieutenant-colonels, and
uniform.

BOOK V. The king comes forward and defies Napoleon to single combat. Napoleon accepts it. Sacri-
fices are offered. The ground is measured by Ney
and Macdonald. The combatants advance. Louis
snaps his pistol in vain. The bullet of Napoleon, on the
contrary, carries off the tip of the king's ear. Napoleon
then rushes on him sword in hand. But Louis snatches
up a stone, such as ten men of those degenerate days
will be unable to move, and hurls it at his antagonist.
Mars averts it. Napoleon then seizes Louis, and is
about to strike a fatal blow, when Bacchus intervenes,
like Venus in the third book of the Illiad, bears off the
king in a thick cloud, and seats him in an hotel at
Lille, with a bottle of Maraschino and a basin of soup
before him. Both armies instantly proclaim Napoleon
emperor.

BOOK VI. Neptune, returned from his Ethiopian
revels, sees with rage the events which have taken
place in Europe. He flies to the cave of Alecto
and drags out the fiend, commanding her to excite

universal hostility against Napoleon. The Fury repairs to Lord Castlereagh ; and as, when she visited Turnus, she assumed the form of an old woman, she here appears in the kindred shape of Mr. Vansittart, and in an impassioned address exhorts his lordship to war.

His Lordship, like Turnus, treats this unwonted monitor with great disrespect, tells him that he is an old doting fool, and advises him to look after the ways and means and leave questions of peace and war to his betters. The Fury then displays all her terrors. The neat powdered hair bristles up into snakes ; the black stockings appear clotted with blood ; and brandishing a torch, she announces her name and mission. Lord Castlereagh, seized with fury, flies instantly to the Parliament, and recommends war with a torrent of eloquent invective. All the members instantly clamor for vengeance, seize their arms which are hanging round the walls of the house, and rush forth to prepare for instant hostilities.

Book VII. In this book, intelligence arrives at London of the flight of the Duchess d'Angoûleme from France. It is stated that this heroine, armed from head to foot, defended Bordeaux against the adherents of Napoleon, and that she fought hand to hand with Clausel, and beat him down with an enormous stone. Deserted by her followers, she at last, like Turnus, plunged, armed as she was, into the Garonne, and swam to an English ship which lay off the coast. This intelligence yet more inflames the English to war.

A yet bolder flight than any which has been mentioned follows. The Duke of Wellington goes to take leave of the duchess ; and a scene passes quite equal to the famous interview of Hector and Andromache. Lord Douro is frightened at his father's feather, but begs for his epaulette.

BOOK VIII. Neptune, trembling for the event of the war, implores Venus, who as the offspring of his element, naturally venerates him, to procure from Vulcan a deadly sword and a pair of unerring pistols for the Duel. They are accordingly made, and superbly decorated. The sheath of the sword, like the shield of Achilles, is carved in exquisitely fine miniature, with scenes from the common life of the period ; a dance at Almack's, a boxing match at the Fives-court, a lord mayor's procession, and a man hanging. All these are fully and elegantly described. The Duke thus armed hastens to Brussels.

BOOK IX. The Duke is received at Brussels by the King of the Netherlands, with great magnificence.

He is informed of the approach of the armies of all the confederate kings. The poet, however, with a laudable zeal for the glory of his country, completely passes over the exploits of the Austrians in Italy, and the discussion of the congress. England and France, Wellington and Napoleon, almost exclusively occupy his attention. Several days are spent at Brussels in revelry. The English heroes astonish their allies by exhibiting splendid games, similar to those which draw the flower of the British aristocracy to Newmarket and Moulsey Hurst, and which will be considered by our descendants with as much veneration as the Olympian and Isthmian contests by classical students of the present time. In the combat of the cestus, Shaw, the life-guardsman, vanquishes the Prince of Orange, and obtains a bull as a prize. In the horse-race, the Duke of Wellington and Lord Uxbridge ride against each other ; the Duke is victorious, and is rewarded with twelve opera-girls. On the last day of the festivities, a splendid dance takes place, at which all the heroes attend.

BOOK X. Mars, seeing the English army thus inactive, hastens to rouse Napoleon, who, conducted by Night and Silence, unexpectedly attacks the Prussians. The slaughter is immense. Napoleon kills many whose histories and families are happily particularized. He slays Herman, the craniologist, who dwelt by the linden-shadowed Elbe, and measured with his eye the skulls of all who walked through the streets of Berlin. Alas! his own skull is now cleft by the Corsican sword. Four pupils of the University of Jena advance together to encounter the Emperor ; at four blows he destroys them all. Blucher rushes to arrest the devastation ; Napoleon strikes him to the ground, and is on the point of killing him, but Gneisenau, Ziethen, Bulow, and all the other heroes of the Prussian army, gather round him and bear the venerable chief to a distance from the field. The slaughter is continued till night. In the mean time Neptune has despatched Fame to bear the intelligence to the Duke, who is dancing at Brussels. The whole army is put in motion. The Duke of Brunswick's horse speaks to admonish him of his danger, but in vain.

BOOK XI. Picton, the Duke of Brunswick, and the Prince of Orange, engage Ney at Quatre Bras. Ney kills the Duke of Brunswick, and strips him, sending his belt to Napoleon. The English fall back on Waterloo. Jupiter calls a council of the gods, and commands that none shall interfere on either side. Mars and Neptune made very eloquent speeches. The battle of Waterloo commences. Napoleon kills Picton and Delancy. Ney engages Ponsonby and kills him. The Prince of Orange is wounded by Soult. Lord Uxbridge flies to check the carnage. He is severely wounded by Napoleon, and only saved by the assistance of Lord Hill. In the mean time the Duke makes a tremendous carnage among the French. He encounters General Duhesme and vanquishes him, but spares his life. He kills Toubert, who kept the gaming-house in the Palais Royal, and Maronet, who loved to spend whole nights in drinking champagne. Clerval, who had been hooted from the stage, and had then become a captain in the Imperial Guard, wished that he had still continued to face the more harmless enmity of the Parisian pit. But Larre, the son of Esculapius, whom his father had instructed in all the secrets of his art, and who was surgeon-general of the French army, embraced the knees of the destroyer, and conjured him not to give death to one whose office it was to give life. The Duke raised him, and bade him live.

But we must hasten to the close. Napoleon rushes to encounter Wellington. Both armies stand in mute amaze. The heroes fire their pistols ; that of Napoleon misses, but that of Wellington, formed by the hand of Vulcan, and primed by the Cyclops, wounds the Emperor in the thigh. He flies, and takes refuge among his troops. The flight becomes promiscuous. The arrival of the Prussians, from a motive of patriotism, the poet completely passes over.

BOOK XII. Things are now hastening to the catastrophe. Napoleon flies to London, and seating himself on the hearth of the Regent, embraces the household gods, and conjures him, by the venerable age of George III., and by the opening perfections of the Princess Charlotte to spare him. The Prince is inclined to do so ; when, looking on his breast he sees there the belt of the Duke of Brunswick. He instantly draws his sword and is about to stab the destroyer of his kinsman. Piety and hospitality, however, restrain his hand. He takes a middle course, and condemns Napoleon to be exposed on a desert island. The king of France re-enters Paris ; and the poem concludes.

THOMAS B. MACAULAY.

ST. TWEL'MO;

OR, THE

Cuneiform Cyclopedist of Chattanooga.

ARGUMENT.

It will perhaps be complained that in this story the Author "aims at nothing." If so, let me reply, in his behalf, that if he hits it he will be perfectly satisfied.

Originally, I intended to address myself only to the half-educated idiots of the land who are unfamiliar with the Coptic and do not take dictionaries with them into the country by way of light summer reading. But if the learned are attracted to my net, so much the better—all is fish. In the outset I own to an endeavor to catch a spark of St. Elmo's fire—there's nothing mean about me. As old Thomas Fuller quaintly puts it, "Let my candle go out in a stink when I refuse to confess from whom I have lighted it." If it be further urged that not content with a spark, I have in some instances raked the entire hearth, I fear I must still plead guilty to the charge. For where it was impossible to pile on the agony of erudition, I took whole pages as well as paragraphs, from the original, dispensing with quotation remarks. If it be complained that, in consequence, the reader can not tell where the original ends and travesty begins, certainly a higher compliment, or a more complete justification of purpose could not fall to my lot.

JOHN PAUL

CHAPTER I.

 T. TWEL'MO was an extraordinary character, living under the shadow of Lookout Mountain.

Whether he lived there because of the blind fumbling of Atheistic Chance, or in accordance with a rigid edict of Pantheistic Necessity, will never be known to any one ; but it is quite likely that necessity had something to do with it, since it is otherwise impossible to understand why a man should live so far from civilization—and so near Chattanooga !

Eccentricities may have compelled him to seek this retirement, for it is quite certain that a man of his manners would have been tolerated in no respectable society ; and had he attempted to pitch his tent further north, the catholic chances are that he would have been speedily committed to an asylum for the insane.

8

Southern gentlemen generally are given to stock raising; but under the shadow of Lookout Mountain St. Twel'mo gathered about him some of the most extraordinary horned cattle that ever were seen in a farm-yard. Instead of dun cows from Durham, he imported a white cow from Ava, utterly regardless of expense and the remonstrance of the negress dairy-maid (the beast, had no milk-giving medium) that she should much prefer "an udder kine."

Then there were reindeer from Lapland, walruses from the cold Arctic seas, goats from Cashmere, (which were mere goats after all), chamois from the Jungfrau, gorillas and guerillas from Central Africa and Missouri, and pelicans from Louisiana.

These, with the polecat, native to the State, furnished him fragrant food for reflection and employment of his leisure hours. Swearing and stirring up the animals were the only amusements in which he indulged, quoting poetry and rudeness to his mother constituting the serious business of his life.

He was accustomed to speak of his *menage;* but the uneducated whites of the district understood the term only as an abbreviation of "menagerie." It is little wonder that they roundly swore, in the vernacular of that region, that St. Twel'mo had "the *dog*-gonedest · and the *ding*-stavingest and the *rip*-snortingest queerest cattle, that ever one *sot* eyes on ! "

For all his cattle, however, and his fifteen acres of pasture, St. Twel'mo could not be called a "gentleman-farmer." For, besides swearing at his mother, he had a habit of yelling ha ! ha ! at young ladies, and lighting cheap cigars in their presence without asking them if they " objected to smoking," practices in which gentlemen, whether farmers or not, never indulge.

But I am managing my story very inartistically. Let me introduce the heroine.

Etna Early was another singular character ; and I may as well remark, right here, that Lookout Mountain must be continually in labor with queer characters as well as with queer cattle, for certainly it brings forth nothing else, if cotemporary history may be relied on.

At the hour and minute at which our story opens, Etna was carrying a pail of water upon her head, which will fully account for the " classic Caryatides" attitudes for which she afterwards became famous, as

well as for the symptoms of " water on the brain "
which she exhibited at times in the course of her
subsequent brilliant career.   And while she carried
she sang, waking the echoes of Lookout with the
chaunt of A Bucket.

Etna's occupation at the moment of introduction
was fortunate ; it enabled her to turn pail and throw
cold water upon a duel over which she happened to
stumble, too late to prevent a fatal consummation to
one of the parties, and not early enough, unfortunately,
to ensure the drowning of both.   However, she was
quite in time to deliver a lecture on the sinfulness
of duelling, to which, as might have been expected,
only the dead man turned an ear, neither of the
seconds having a minute to spare, and the sur-
viving principal having another engagement on hand.

The next, and perhaps a more important epoch in
Etna's life, was her discovery of a dictionary, though
how such a thing got under the shadow of Lookout Mountain only the Lord and the colporteurs
know.   This was worse than the duel ; it proved, in
fact, a triple calamity, for she acquired in consequence a fatal fondness for polysyllables, a trick of
speaking them trippingly and a contempt for common English, from which she never recovered.

CHAPTER II.

HAD forgotten to mention that Etna had a grandfather, Aaron Hunt, a blacksmith, a useful, and withal a rather sensible man; reasons enough, and too many, why he should be dismissed from the story and buried under the shadow of Lookout Mountain at the earliest possible moment.

On this occasion Etna, accompanied by her dog "Grip" (his name was Agrippa—and so was he, as many a school-boy could testify to his sorrow), was skipping along the path that led to the shop. On the way she encountered a solitary horseman, who asked her if there was a blacksmith in the vicinity —his horse had lost a shoe.

With that keen eye to business which everywhere forms an element of the feminine character, Etna replied that her grandfather was in the "profession," and was counted the best "tharabout," pointing the stranger so plainly to the shop that he could only wilfully blunder upon the forge of a rival.

Arrived at the smithy, she found the stranger already there, a natural result of his being on horseback and her on foot. Not at all regardful of the fact that work was on the anvil, and that the stranger was waiting, she seated herself on a keg of nails and asked her grandfather whether he thought Jupiter treated Juno exactly right in the matter. of Io; for she had not yet encountered a full-grown classical dictionary, and scarcely knew IO even by sight. Her mistake in this instance may, perhaps, be set down to a Ten-nes-see education.

With that ingenuousness and inattention to business for which old age is sometimes remarkable, Aaron dropped the horse's hoof from his lap and proceeded to discuss the mythology in all its bearings and interpretations.

The stranger waxed as wroth with this Aaron, under the shadow of Lookout Mountain, as did Moses with the old-time Aaron under the shadow of Sinai; and scowled and stamped and clamored to have his horse shod. But it was impossible to

quench Etna when eruptive with erudition, and still
the lava of learning flowed from the "cratur's"
mouth.

" Dog-gone Jupiter and Io ! How much do *I* owe
you?" shouted the stranger at last, flinging a gold
dollar down in the tall grass and galloping away
with his fingers in his ears.*

" He is a rude, blasphemous, wicked man," said
Aaron Hunt, after hunting for the coin an hour or
two without finding it. " I don't care for the dollar,"
he added, as he returned his spectacles to his pocket
and lit his pipe at the forge, " but I would mainly
like to know where the darned thing got to. "

Etna continued the search. It was vain so far as
finding the money was concerned ; but judge of her
surprise and. delight when she found, on the stranger's late stamping-ground, an Unabridged Webster's
Dictionary, a complete set of the Cyclopedia Britan-
nica, Piper's Operative Surgery, and a Dictionary
of Familiar Quotations. On the fly-leaf of one of
the volumes was printed " 12mo," and on that of the
" Unabridged," *Lasciaogui speranzi voi ch' entrate.*

Turning to the book of quotations, she found that
the phrase was translated, " Who enters here leaves
Hope behind."

Seating herself on the grass, she committed to memory all the big words of the Dictionary, and half the contents of the Cyclopedia, before sundown. Returning home, she found her grandfather peacefully smoking a pipe at his cottage door.

" Welcome, my child, " said he, " come, tell me how you have amused yourself this bright, beautiful afternoon."

" Aged grandsire," replied the child, "to plunge *in medias res*, inaugurating my narration without an appogiatura ; touching the origin of the infusoria, Leuwenhoek, Gleichen, Zenzis-Khan, Alexander, Attila, Gurowski, to say nothing of the iridiscent *Illuminati* of Boston (this last was spoken sarcastically, for Etna was a true Southern girl), all entertain different opinions. Also, in the course of varied studies, I observe with regret that, as regards the Rhinoplastic or Taliacotian operation, as to whether the cellular tissue should be dissected down to the periosteum, leaving the *os humerus* or lumbar region to infringe upon the pericardium, to the disarrangement and displacement of the *arbor vitæ*, chirurgeons differ, nor are they even united as to the best method of demephitization ; ischuretics also are still a matter of dispute. And when chirurgeons who have passed beyond the stormy esophagus of science and gained the smooth Bahr-Shei-tan beyond (here "Grip" barked) differ by so much as a dodecatemorion, who shall decide? You may, *par example*, imagine that, because I am a woman, I have no right to express an opinion thus freely and *con amore;* but, is woman merely an *adscriptus glebæ* chameleon-like— but here I will explain that the old theory about the chameleon taking its hue from—

"O grandy! what's the matter?"

For she now noticed that the old man's head reclined peacefully on his breast.

Alas! as Etna expressed it in her diary, Aaron Hunt had "passed to everlasting repose." As a gambling friend of the family told it at the tavern that evening, somewhat more tersely, he had "passed in his chips."

To put it in plain English, he was dead. The appogiatura staggered him some, but the dodecatemorion knocked him cold as a wedge.

Quite satisfied with the result of her first experiment, Etna packed her dictionaries and cyclopdias and her dog "Grip," and started by the next train from Chattanooga.

CHAPTER III.

IT seems that they have a branch of the Camden and Amboy railroad down in Tennessee.

There was a smash and a crash of silver cords and golden bowls, and china soup tureens, and other crockery, a blind fumbling to save the pieces, cherry beams and butternut timbers dropped down on the astonished passengers, and Etna was rudely snatched from the banks of Bahr-Sheitan, whereon she basked in a delicious dream, to find herself buried under dead bodies and dictionaries and car wheels and cord wood which had fallen on her in the general wreck and ruin.

"The kind and gentlemanly conductor" came around to look after the tickets. Spying Etna, stand-

ing on her head with her feet sticking out of the rub-
bish, he inquired, with a polite bow, if he could do
any thing for her. She said yes; that sundry im-
pedimenta excoriated her cuticle and that it was impossible for her to recalcitrate. He understood the
trouble at once, and replied, "Certainly with pleasure," swinging his lantern three times round his head
—a signal which all the world over is understood to
mean "down brakes." Men came rushing from all
sides, and after two hours' dry digging *à la grec*, by
two stout Irishmen with shovels, Etna was excavated.
She had sustained some slight injuries—a dislocated
shoulder, broken ankles, and a few shattered tibia—
but not enough to prevent her from entering into
cheerful conversation with the surgeon, discussing
cartilaginous capsules, provisional calli, and repara-
tion of fractures in a fashion which astonished, if it
did not enlighten that worthy man.

Having exhausted her subjects and the surgeon,
first she inquired for her dictionary, and then for her
dog.

The dictionary, somewhat scraped and dusty, but
otherwise quite uninjured, was placed in her hands.
Clasping it to her heart, she expressed a desire that
it should be buried with her in event of her injuries

terminating fatally ; its presence, she said was necessary to her " everlasting repose."

On being told that her dog was dead, she manifested much emotion and wept bitterly. It was plain
to the most casual observer that the poor girl had
lost her Grip.

Indeed it was a terrible scene, waterfalls, lunch-
baskets, bird-cages, and hoop-skirts were piled up on
all sides in the most promiscuous confusion.

A middle-dressed, elegantly-aged lady, who was
fumbling around in the *débris* for her false teeth,
found Etna. She had previously overheard her conversation with the surgeon.

"Bless my soul !" cried she, "here is a girl of
twelve talking like a long-bearded rabbi ; here
is another curiosity for the bear-garden." And
she whisked Etna away to her chateau, known
thereabout as Le Beaucage, which lay conveniently
near.

The lady was St. Twel'mo's mother, and her name
was Murray.

With the proud independence of a noble nature,
Etna refused to accept the home which was offered her,
unless permitted to "pay for it." This Mrs. Murray would not allow—one reason of her refusing to

"take any thing" being that the orphan had nothing to give. She agreed to "charge it," however, which, in some degree, satisfied Etna's scruples, and reconciled her to become a permanent fixture of Le Beaucage.

CHAPTER IV.

ETNA'S first introduction to St. Twel'mo happened in this wise:

She was seated in her bedroom one morning in earnest conversation with Mrs. Murray. The discourse was about board, lodgings, and music-lessons; and Etna having pledged her word to pay nothing for any thing until she had some thing to pay with, Mrs. Murray was delighted, and embraced her *sur l'œil gauche*, in a very fervent fashion.

Suddenly the door opened, and a "gentleman" strode into the room, carrying a bag of game. At sight of Etna, he stopped, dropped his dead ducks and snipe on the floor, and shouted:

"What the devil does this mean?"

Had Etna then possessed that coolness and *savoir faire* which she acquired later in life, she might have replied to the rude conundrum by pro-

pounding one much more impertinent. Pointing to
the mess on the floor, she might have asked :

"Is that your Little Game?"

But it is recorded of her on this occasion that she
spoke not a single syllable. Indeed, she was never
much given to single syllables, rarely, at any period .
of her career, troubling her lips with a word of less
than five.

Mrs. Murray having explained that the young lady
was one of the sufferers by the late disaster, picked
up the game-bag, and taking her son affectionately
by the arm, led him from the room, without giving
him a chance to apologize for his rudeness.

Had he been led out by the nose, he would have
had no more than his desert, and scarcely that ; but
mark you how Etna was affected.

A thrill shot along her nerves ; she felt a blind
fumbling at her heart-strings ; a presentiment overwhelmed her ; the Pantheistic Necessity that she
should marry the rude intruder became evident and
apparent—in him she recognized the coming man.

The coming man—that is, the one who had just
gone out—was tall and athletic, not exactly young
and not precisely elderly ; it would be safe to set
him down as middle-aged. According to all accounts,

he must have been a rather rum-looking **customer**;
for his fair chiselled lineaments were spotted by dissipation and blackened and distorted by the baleful
fires of a fierce, passionate nature, and a restless,
powerful, and unhallowed intellect. Furthermore,
he was symmetrical and grand

> As some temple of Juno,
>   Whose polished shafts
> Gleam'd centuries ago,
>   In the morning sunshine
> Of a day of wo

(this thing resolves itself into rhyme), whose untimely
night has endured for nineteen hundred years; so in
the glorious flush of his youth this man had stood
facing a noble and possibly sanctified future (and
things); but the ungovernable flames of sin had
reduced him, like that blackened and desecrated
fane, to a melancholy mass of ashy arches and blackened columns, where ministering priests, all holy
aspirations, slumbered in the dust.

The dress of this melancholy mass of ashy arches
and blackened columns was costly but negligent, and
the red stain on his jacket told that his errand had
not been fruitless (from which it might be inferred

that he had been strawberrying as well as ducking).
As part of this costly but negligent dress, the melancholy mass wore a straw hat belted with broad black
ribbons, and his spurred boots (hunters down there
always put spurs on when they chase the wild duck
and the fierce snipe to their Lookout Mountain fast-
nesses) were damp and muddy.

It seems rather melancholy, at first glance, that
this melancholy mass of mud and ministering priests,
and arches and columns, and spurs and straw hats,
and broad black ribbons, should demean itself in the
way he did, striding into a young lady's bed-chamber,
dumping dead ducks on the carpet, braying out Ha!
ha! like Mephistopheles in the play or a jackass in
a corn-field, and asking, "What the devil does this
mean?" of its own mother. Indeed, nothing but a
blackened column or a negro minstrel could do such
things without a blush.

Something in the column's tones—I almost said
the column's base—recalled to Etna's memory the
rude, wicked, blasphemous man who said, "Dog-
gone it!" to her grandfather, and left dictionaries
and cyclopedias lying around loose on the grass before the shop.

She could hear him in the next room, talking to
9

his mother. He called her *" ma mère "* (perhaps the least objectionable way in which he could dam her) and Etna an ancolyte, prophesying that some day the latter would turn up *non est,* ditto silver forks, ditto diamonds, ditto gold spoons.

Etna all this while felt the indignant blood burning her cheeks ; but having plenty of cheek and to spare, she simply let it burn on, and sat and heard the conversation through. At the doubts expressed of her honesty, she started ; for she remembered the dictionaries and cyclopedias of the smithy, for which she had never endeavored to find an owner, and she wondered whether St. Twel'mo remembered them too. Feeling rather apprehensive that he might recognize them if they fell in his way, she determined to return them in the morning.

But in the morning an unforeseen accident occurred. Going out on the lawn, to play with the elephants, and rhinoceroses, and pelicans, a huge dog came tearing along, and after biting off an elephant's ear, and strangling a rhinoceros or two, turned on Etna.

Faint with terror, she was incapable of lifting a hand in her defense, and even forgot to quote—the first time in life that she ever missed an opportunity.

It galled her afterwards to think how patly she could have put in the lines of Dr. Watts, beginning

" Let dogs delight to bark and bite ; "

but the circumstances were not favorable for classic indulgences.

Of course St. Twel'mo came on opportunely and called off his dog. He did more, he picked up a club and belabored the dog, which howled, and St. Twel'mo howled, and the rhinoceros bellowed, while Etna, fully restored to a sense of her mission in life, mounted a stump and chanted the prayer of Habakkuk in the original Hebrew, so that altogether they had a very effective quartet and quite a lively and interesting time of it.

And after it was all over, and St. Twel'mo had done licking the dog, the dog, probably thinking that one good turn deserved another, turned and licked his master's feet, which gave St. Twel'mo an opportunity to cry Ha ! and remark that that was the way of all natures, human as well as brute.

MEM. The behavior of the dog in the *finale* of this matter leads me to the inevitable conclusion that it was a female dog.

I mean no disrespect to the sex by the preceding annotation ; I simply mean that such would be the logical deduction did we accept the heroines of most women's novels as types of womanhood at large. For here was St. Twel'mo, whose face was blotted with dissipation, and blackened and distorted by baleful fires, and who looked like a melancholy mass of ashy arches and blackened columns, and who was always damning his mother and his sweethearts, and crying ha ! to them, and saying *par parenthèse*, and *par excellence*, and *par exemple*, and *par nobile fratrum*, and *parbleu*—

(His French and his Latin were seldom or never above par)—

Yet carrying innumerable female scalps at his belt. How such a fellow could win the affections of refined and cultivated women, I cannot understand. For I have tried original verses, and pet names, and bouquets, and gentlemanly behavior, and the sweet influences of modest and unpretending merit, all in vain.

The moral that women with "intellect into them," can be best won by pelting them with vituperation and junk-bottles instead of with bon-bons, and telling them to go to the devil instead of to Delmonico's where any thing they choose to fancy in the way of lunch awaits them, I do not believe, and do here resolutely refuse to accept, though all the authoresses in Christendom and out of it are leagued together to persuade me to the contrary ; after which personal explanation I resume the thread of my story.

CHAPTER V.

HE same evening Etna determined to call at St. Twe!'mo's apartments—notwithstanding the injunction from all about the house that she must never cross the threshold of his room—and return the dictionaries and cyclopedias.

As already remarked, it was the evening of the day on which the encounter with the dog occurred. By some strange fumbling or thimble-rigging of the planets, Sirius was just wagging its tail in the eastern horizon, when Etna knocked at the terrible doors.

Was it an omen? Was the dog-star indeed to prove the star of her destiny?

Rat! tat! tat!

Etna executed the long roll which a woman beats, echoing her heart-taps, when in doubt as to the propriety of a step, but has already determined to "go in," cost what it may.

"Come in!"

The voice was gruff as that of the wolf in reply to Red Riding Hood's tattoo.

She opened the door and waited for a second invitation. It came.

" Come in, damn you ! " growled the inmate, blowing the smoke of a very bad cigar, which smelt like brimstone, in scattered spirals to the vaulted and fluted ceiling.

On this she entered. St. Twel'mo did not rise, and the tableau was a peculiar one. There sat our hero, gaunt and peculiar. The peculiarity of the gaunt look which enveloped him, as with a mantle, is readily enough explained when we consider " that for nearly fifteen dreary years, nothing but jeers, and oaths, and sarcasms, had crossed his finely sculptured lips." It is little wonder that on such diet he had not fleshed up much ; but it is indeed singular that some of the oaths and things had not strangled him.

The reflection occurs that he must at times have felt thirsty ; but perhaps, like the lover mentioned in the lyric, he drank only with his eyes. A hypothesis which is strengthened by the fact that it was out from his glowing gray eyes that the mocking demon of the wine-cup looked.

But to resume. On his swarthy and colorless

face, midnight orgies and habitual excesses had left their unmistakable plague spot, and Mephistopheles had stamped his signet. Is it any wonder that Etna's love fed as she gazed, and that, lost in contemplation of the pleasant picture, and a possibly bright future before her, she wholly forgot the errand which brought her thither?

" What the devil does this mean, and what do you want?" growled St. Twel'mo. " Squattez vous lá," and he pointed to a chair.

" No, I thank you," replied Etna with a graceful courtesy, " I only come to return some books I borrowed of you."

And turning to a black servant who stood behind her with a hand cart, she bade him wheel it in.

He obeyed, and she rapidly began to unload it of dictionaries and cyclopedias. With a sudden expression of interest in his countenance, the master of the apartment rose from his gracefully recumbent position and approached her.

" In the name of the Great Horned Dromedary of Eblis, whose hump, bright with the glitter of eternal snows, gleams across the northern horizon at midnight, and is mistaken by sciolists and the half-educated idiots, who at that time burnt expensive kerosene in a vain attempt to review books which they can not understand, for the *aurora borealis*—the origin of which phenomenon I have not time just now to explain—tell me what is this mystery ? "

He took the huge volume "mechanically"—that is by the aid of a derrick, which was rigged up at that end of the apartment, and his stern swarthy face lighted up joyfully.

" Is it possible ? my dear Unabridged ! the very copy that has travelled round the world in my vest pocket, and without which I was lost. Can it be ? Tell me, girl, where did you get it ?"

She explained the circumstances as well as she could. But lost in rapture as he rapidly turned over its well-thumbed pages, he bade no heed to her words.

Suddenly his brow darkened, his eye flashed, and his nostrils dilated, as turning to her in a voice of thunder, he roared :

" Damnation ! you have stolen all the big words out of it ! *Bithus contra Bacchium !* Get out of this !"

Sorrowfully thinking what a pity it was that such a noble intellect, and such an ornament to society should be lost to the world, Etna turned and left the apartment.

As she turned a corner in the corridor, St. Twel'mo, with a Dutch oath, which unfortunately she could not understand, hurled the dictionary at her; missing her fragile form, it struck a plaster bust of Lord Chesterfield which stood in range, inflicting several compound fractures which no plaster could mend. The back of the book was also bust. Cyclopedias and yellow-covered novels came hurling after. Safe in the sanctuary of a convenient closet, Etna dropped upon her knees and softly murmured, " Who smote the marble gods of Greece ? "

St. Twel'mo howling his favorite slogans, *Bithus contra Bacchium* and *Chacun à son goût*, rushed into his solitary apartments, slammed the doors behind him, and spent the rest of the night in horrible dissipation over a small Jenkins's Vest Pocket Dictionary, but it consoled him not for the loss of his Unabridged.

ETNA'S curiosity was awakened by the glimpse she had obtained of bachelor quarters, and she determined to explore them at her leisure, immediately an opportunity offered.

She had not long to wait. The next day St. Twel'mo mounted his horse and galloped over to Chattanooga to purchase a spelling book, for which he had need in writing a business letter to a greasy mechanic who had agreed to construct a hydraulic ram on the premises for the benefit of the Merino sheep, and Cashmere goats—the poor creatures suffered sadly from want of an adequate supply of water.

No sooner had the echoing tramp of his horse's hoofs died away in the distance, than Etna installed herself in the vacant rooms, and made herself perfectly at home.

Indeed St. Twel'mo's apartments were curiously furnished. In lieu of sofas, and ottomans, and Turkish chairs, and meerschaums, and spittoons, and photograph albums, and coal-scuttles, and handsomely bound copies of Liffith Lank, and The Jumping Frog, and boxing-gloves, and foils, and cheese-toasters, and tailors' bills, and old boots, and embroidered slippers, and dressing-gowns, and cigar-stumps, and soda water, and empty bottles, and portraits of popular actresses, and other things that men's rooms are generally full of, she found only old vases and antique jars—family jars—of no possible use, not even to "sit down" on; and cameos, and cameras, and intaglios, and entanglements, and prospectuses of new gas companies for supplying the pyramids with cheap light, and Turcoman cimetars—croocked as rams' horns—Bedouin lances, Bowie knives, flint-lock muskets, and other queer weapons which afterwards contributed so largely to the armament of the Confederate forces. Besides, there was an astonishing pile of cyclopedias, dictionaries, languages without masters and masters without languages, a volume entitled A Thousand Things Worth Knowing, and a whole library which might have been labelled, *not* Worth Knowing! More things, in fact, were in these bachelor's quarters—he never did things by halves—than Horatio or even the fanciful Philes ever dreamed of in their Philosophies.

But what most attracted Etna's attention was one of those mysterious contrivances known as a "Herring's Safe," whether because a herring in them is safe from roasting or sure to be done to a turn, no philologist has yet proclaimed. It was modeled after a miracle of Saracenic architecture, and had a lock which defied gunpowder, and extemporized keys made of crooked nails ; the door was painted to resemble live oak, but the inscription thereon was written in a dead language.

Etna would have liked to know what the thing contained, but the combination-lock refused to respond to the pass-keys she carried about her, and all her blind fumbling at the mystic key-hole proved of no avail.

She sighed and wished that her grandfather was around with his sledge-hammer.

As she turned away and retraced her steps among the costly *bizarrerie* it suddenly occurred to her that no light childish feet had ever pattered down the long rows of shining tiles, and she suddenly thought " What a pity, oh ! if——"

(Why do such things always occur to women when men never think of them ?)

And then, with a sorrowful sigh, she sought her

own apartment. Her dreams that night were of wedding favors—sometimes written "fevers" by the illiterate—and the altar assumed the shape of a burglar and fire-proof safe.

Pressing her lips closely to the open end of the bolster, under the natural but mistaken impression that it was the happy bridegroom's ear, she whispered softly, "Ducky, deary, *what* on earth *do* you keep in that big iron bandbox?"

O the days wore on at Le Beaucage—and that every thing did not wear out was very strange indeed And Etna progressed in knowledge. In company with a fine and erudite old clergyman, named Gammon, she committed to memory nearly all the books which no gentleman's library should be without, all the quotable passages in Diodorus, Tupper, Owen Meredith, Mark Twain, Plutarch, John Ruskin, Charles Algernon Swinburne, Thucydides, and Walt Whitman. For she had made up her mind to go forth and face the world—outface it, if necessary.

The only subject on which there was not full sympathy and perfect communion between Etna and the Rev. Mr. Gammon was that *mauvais sujet*, St. Twel'mo. Etna feared that her tutor did not love her hero, and one day asked him how? and if not, wherefore? The reverend gentleman clasped his hands and declared that he loved St. Twel'mo as well as his own life, if not better. At first

Etna would not believe this declaration, but when she learned that St. Twel'mo had murdered a couple of the clergyman's children, she gave it implicit credence. For she herself had not been entreated over and above well at his hands, and the seething of love in her own heart in consequence convinced her that some pork would boil so—pardon the homeliness of the proverb.

If I have until now forgotten to mention one peculiarity about St. Twel'mo, let me at once remedy the omission. He was wonderfully fond of travel, the result, perhaps, of his pedigree. For his father, also named Murray, was none other than the illustrious author of those guide books, so familiar and famous all Europe through. The mistaken impression which obtained on some sides, that he was descended from Lindley Murray, St. Twel'mo denounced with disdain, proudly boasting that there was never a grammarian in the family—a fact too patent to be gainsaid by any.

Impatient of home and never at rest, his footsteps had sounded among the steppes of Tartary; Arabs on the great desert were acquainted with his war-cry of *Bithus contra Bacchium;* Fejee chieftains, while breakfasting on underdone missionary, had been

made familiar with his favorite apophthegm, *Chacun
à son goût.* As an explorer of equatorial Africa, he
divided the honors with Du Chaillu, and was certainly entitled to the odd trick, for it could not be denied
that he brought home with him more of the habits
and manners of the gorillas than Du Chailla did. In
short, there was only one spot on the face of the
earth which he had not visited—that was the State
of New-Jersey. And one morning, at the breakfast
table, he announced to his mother his intention of
making a journey thither. With a wild shriek, she
dropped the tea-pot from her hand, and was carried
away from the table upon the tray.

Without minding the old lady at all, he strode out
to the stable, ordered his horse saddled and some
pork and hominy packed up, and galloped away.

After galloping as far as the gate, he paused
turned and beckoned to Etna. She approached
him. Drawing a huge key from his pocket, he told
her that it belonged to the big safe—he called it *Taj
Mahal*, which is Dutch for Red Herring—informed
her that the safe contained papers of no value to
any one but the owner, and of very little to him,
and that he intended to intrust the key to her
care. But he forbade her opening it unless he was
10

four years absent, in which event she might conclude
that he had been elected governor and would never
more return.

Etna pertinently remarked that if she was not allowed to use the safe to keep her chignon, and hair-
pins, and pearl-powder in, she didn't see what use
there was in leaving her the key ; but finally consented to accept the trust, sagely saying to herself
that very possibly it might turn to some account.

He plunged spurs in his horse and was gone.

Etna at once returned to the house and examined
the safe.   A small spider had crawled into the key-
hole, and thinking he might injure the lock, she put
in the key and turned it gently, to drive him out.
She was afraid that the door might accidentally
open ; but no—the bolt was rusty and refused to
stir ; for fifteen years it had known no other assuage-
ment of fiction than oaths, and jeers, and sarcasms
—in which respect it resembled St. Twel'mo's lips.

After turning for an hour or two, she finally turned
away, and buried herself in a reprint of the Bhagvat-
Geeta, just republished by Philes.   The Targum
had hitherto been her pabulum during solitary moments, but she had chewed upon it so long that she
desired a change.

Suddenly she was recalled from the delicious dialogues of Kreeshna and Arjoon by a mellow voice under the window, singing:

" I will chase the elephant over the plain,
The rhinoceros I'll bind with a chain,
And the hippopotamus, with his silvery feet,
I'll give thee for a playmate sweet."

Approaching the window, she recognized Gordon Lee, a distant relative of the general of that name who was lately presented with a pair of game-cocks. He addressed her a few words in Greek, to which she coyly replied in Coptic. After this cheerful interchange of greetings, she went down and sat with him in the bear-garden in front of the house. They talked of megatheriums, acephala, mastodons, cubic roots, rhomboids, and cognate ideas that the youthful imagination gererally runs riot with of moonlight evenings.

Gordon was a handsome young fellow, well born, well educated, and of good connections—though he missed some of them when the gun-boats were reported as steaming down the river. Courteous to his equals and kind to his inferiors, he was a general favorite in Chattanooga. Etna, and he had studied the Sanskrit together, sitting at the feet of Gamaliel Gammon, (who, like many others of the cloth, was familiar with most languages except English,) and latterly they had been deep in a translation of the Manavad-harmasastra, each trying to distance the other, but so far it had been a tie between them. Now the tie was all on Gordon's side, and so difficult a one was it to undo that it might be called a Gordian knot.   He was in love with Etna, and had wooed her in Chinese, Cufic, Hebrew, and Massachusetts French, but without effect.   Unfortunately for the success of his suit, he was not scorched by baleful fires, nor blotted by dissipation, and didn't look like a ruined temple, nor a dilapidated tar-kiln, nor a melancholy mass of ashy arches, and charcoal pits, and whisky cock-tails.   Besides, he was neat in his dress and respectful to his mother, and didn't quote and swear.   Had he ever seduced a woman, or shot a man, or even robbed a contribution-box, there might have been some chance for him ; but as it was, his case was hopeless.

This evening the moon was mellow and so was Gordon ; for the one had filled her horns and the other had emptied his.   Under these conditions and combinations he had more courage than usual, and skillfully turned the conversation upon trilobites—though musquito bites would have been more *apropos* to the season—as a neat way of approaching the subject which was nearest his heart. He had found one of rare beauty during the day, and begged her acceptance of it ; but she declined on the plea that there was no vacancy in her cabinet. He then besought her acceptance of a ring, taking a California diamond of fabulous value—wholly fabulous—from his pocket.

" It is beautiful in this light," he said, holding it up to the stars, " how it glistens ; do you see it ? "

" Alas ! no, not in those lamps," she replied, and though she finally consented to accept the ring, she gave him definitely to understand that he was out of it.

On returning to the house Etna looked as though she had been doing something foolish, and Mrs. Murray divined the truth. " How could you ? " she cried. " A young man of excellent principles, sound religious convictions, five hundred niggers, not counting piccaninnies, and raising rather more than a bale to the acre ! *How* could you be *so* foolish, and *so* cruel ? "

" Alas ! mamma," sobbed Etna, hiding her face on

Mrs. Murray's bosom. " he mispronounced a **Greek** quantity."

And Mrs. Murray, who knew how sensitive the child was on such points, but did not dream that a deeper reason underlay the refusal, forgave at once, and comforted her with the hope that one of the Harvard professors might yet happen that way, and she could have a husband to her liking.

CHAPTER VIII.

FTER learning that Gordon Lee was spoony on her, it became manifestly necessary that they should no longer study together. Geometry must specially be given up as tending to excite the blood, and there was no telling even what trouble might be Hebrewing if they met upon the plains of that primitive language.

Suddenly a brillant idea occurred to Etna. She would be an authoress. She would elevate her sex, she would write essays, poetry, tales, novels. There were no bounds to her ambition. Clasping her hands—in default of any one else's a woman is apt to clasp her own—she cried, " To what may I not in time aspire? Even Godey's Lady's Book is not beyond my reach !"

Down there the ladies add a syllable to the favorite oath of the sterner sex, and swear by Godey. It is so easy to understand, and has so many pretty pictures.

"Yes," mused Etna, "the true end and aim of woman's life should be to write a novel." And immediately she seated herself at her escritoire, and wrote to all the editors in New-York, Boston, and Philadelphia, inclosing to each a few hundred pages of MS., and requesting an insertion in their next numbers.

Pending replies, St. Twel'mo came home.

The first question he asked—before even swearing at his mother—was of Etna.

"Have you opened the Taj Mahal?"

"No," she replied.

Of course he intimated with his usual courtesy that she lied, and dragged her off to the library.

She stood trembling while he fumbled at the keyhole. "I know you have opened the door," he exclaimed; "but we will see." Another spider has been at work; with one sweep of his powerful arm he scattered the web to the winds. "If you have not opened it, there will be an explosion," he said.

It occurred to her that there would also be an explosion if she had; but she stood her ground with the calmness befitting one who.aspired to periodical, and was not afraid of magazine.

He swung the door open and a columbiad was

discharged, belching forth its fire and smoke into the room, hoisting St. Twel'mo and Etna to the ceiling, to the dislocation of the latter's waterfall, and so startling her that for the second time in life, she quailed instead of quoting.

St. Twel'mo was so surprised to find that the door had not been opened in his absence to the ignition of his infernal machine, and that Etna was alive, and he was alive, and there was nothing dead in the room but a few languages, that he pulled from his finger a ring, engrossed with a Chaldaic character, and insisted upon her acceptance of it.

Etna's eyes glistened as she gazed upon the jewel and recognized the talismanic sign it bore.

But other visions unfolded themselves to her. Beyond blazed the torch, that *ignis fatuus* which has led so many up the steep and winding stairs of the great white fane in Franklin Square, to find no rest for their feet, nor acceptance of their handiwork when their story reached that third story, known as the Aisle of Guernsey. And over a distant frog pond stood the nebulous

familiar to all who have sought the Philosopher's Tone, and hateful to those who have found it not. And she determined not to be in a hurry about accepting any thing.

With an angry hand he dashed the

into the grate. "The badge of my race," he said; "it will be quite at home among the congenial flames—there at least it will be red. Many a stout Twel'mo has had the same grate circulation," and he laughed savagely.

With the glare of the grate in his face and its smoke in his hair, he looked so supernaturally ugly and so unusually wicked, that Etna's heart warmed toward him, and she hung out that light in her eyes which all the world over is accepted and recognized as the signal for a flirtation. This was seven o'clock in the evening.

About nine o'clock, two hours later, the affair was progressing as follows—St. Twel'mo loquitur:

"Pardon me if I remind you," he said, "of the preliminary and courteous *en garde!* which should be pronounced before a thrust. De Guerin felt

starved in Languedoc, and no wonder! But had
he penetrated every nook and cranny of the habit-
able globe and traversed the Zaharas which science
accords the universe, he would have died at last as
hungry as Ugolino. I speak advisedly, for the true
Io gadfly *ennui* has stung me from hemisphere to
hemisphere, across tempestuous oceans, scorching
deserts, and icy mountain ranges. I have faced
alike the bourrans of the steppes and the Samieli of
Shamo, and the result of my vandal life is best
epitomized in those grand but grim words of Bossuet:
' *On trouve au fond de tout le vide et le néant.*' Nineteen years ago, to satisfy my hunger, I set out to
hunt the daintiest food this world would furnish, and,
like other fools, have learned finally, that life is but
a huge mellow golden Osher, (short for pumpkin,)
that mockingly sifts its bitter dust upon our eager
lips. Ah! truly, *On trouve au fond de tout le vide et
le néant?*" Etna promptly made answer to this
sprightly little sally: "Mr. Murray, if you insist
upon your bitter Osher simile, why shut your eyes to
the palpable analogy suggested? Naturalists assert
that the Solanum, or apple of Sodom, contains in
its normal state neither dust nor ashes, unless it is
punctured by an insect, (the Tenthredo,) which

converts the whole of the inside into dust, leaving nothing but the rind entire, without any loss of color. Human life is as fair and tempting as the fruit of Ain Jidy, till stung and poisoned by the Tenthredo of sin."

"Will you favor me," he replied, "by lifting on the point of your dissecting-knife this stinging sin of mine to which you refer? The noxious brood swarm so teasingly about my ears that they deprive me of your cool, clear, philosophic discrimination. Which particular Tenthredo of the buzzing swarm around my spoiled apple of life would you advise me to select for my *anathema maranatha ?*"

(At this point the servant girl, who was dusting the drawers with a peacock's tail, looked around; for her name was Anna Maria, and she thought she was called.)

"Of your history, sir," returned Etna, "I am entirely ignorant! and even if I were not, I should not presume to levy a tax upon it in discussions with you ; for however vulnerable you may possibly be, I regard an *argumentum ad hominem* (here the servant girl, thinking that hominy was meant and mentioned, brightened up and put on an intelligent look) as the weakest weapon in the army of dialectics—a weapon too——"

But that will do for the present. Suffice it to say that this thing went on for two hours more, and that a full report of the speeches would occupy twenty pages of foolscap, and could only be made tolerable by an accompanying jingle of as many bells. When the little *coquetterie* ended at a time for putting out the lights, both sat asleep in their respective chairs whispering big words in each other's ears from sheer force of habit.

T. TWEL'MO was a decidedly original wooer. Like an Indian chief, the moment he set out on the war path he began to recount how many scalps he had previously taken. Thus, cornering Etna in a church one evening, while she was practicing, in preparation for the next Sunday, upon the hand organ, which did duty in lieu of a larger wind instrument, he breathed a soft confession into her ear.

Printed, I am aware that it will read very much like a page from the Newgate Calendar.

It seemed that a son of the Rev. Mr. Gammon had cut him out with the daughter of another clergyman, by wearing higher shirt collars and indulging more lavishly in pomatums and macassar. A challenge passed between them, and St. Twel'mo killed his antagonist at the first fire.

Thenceforth his career was a strange one, and its

recital must have been edifying to Etna's ears. He
seduced every " brilliant and accomplished woman "
that the village of Chattanooga and the surrounding
swamps contained, "winning her love and then
leaving her a target for the laughter of her circle "—
to be blasted, as it were, by blow-guns. This he told
his sweetheart. " One of the fairest faces that ever
brightened the haunts of fashion—a queenly, elegant
girl—the pet of her family and of society," he seduced
and reduced to a melancholy mass of ashy arches and
things somewhat a-kiln to himself. At the time that
he told this story, she was " wearing serge garments"
in an Italian convent. Serge was her life! St.
Twel'mo was wearing spurred-boots the while, and telling these tales to his sweetheart.

But the exploit on which he most prided himself,
the one he "norated " with the greatest zest, assuming
the half-deprecating air of those excessively virtuous
persons who "do good by stealth and blush to find
it fame," was as follows. The scene occured at the
parsonage, and I allow St. Twel'mo to tell the story
in his own words:

" During one terribly fatal winter, scarlet fever had
deprived the Rev. Mr. Gammon of four children,
(St. Twel'mo and scarlet fever seem to have run in

the family,) leaving him an only daughter, Annie, the image of her brother, (the brother whom he had taken the precaution to kill.)   Her health was feeble; consumption was stretching its skeleton hands toward her, and her father watched her as a gardener tends his pet, choice, delicate exotic.   She was about sixteen, very pretty, very attractive.   After her brother's death, I never spoke to Mr. Gammon, never crossed his path; but I met his daughter without his knowledge, and finally I made her confess her love for me.   I offered her my hand; she accepted it.   A day was appointed for an elopement and marriage; the hour came; she left the parsonage, but I did not meet her here on the steps of this church as I had promised, and she received a note, full of scorn and derision, explaining the revengeful motives that had actuated me.   Two hours later, her father found her insensible on the steps, (she could scarcely have been sensible when she took the step,) and the marble was dripping with a hemorrhage of blood (alas! that it was of *blood*) from her lungs. The dark stain is still there; you must have noticed it.   I never saw her again.   She kept her room (better it must have been than St. Twel'mo's company) from that day, and died three months after.   When on her death-bed she sent for me, but I refused to obey the summons."

The story of our hero's loves and triumphs by no means ended here ; but sufficient for this day is the evil thereof. *Ex pede Herculem*—it is not expedient to prolong the agonies ; the devil, quite as well as Hercules, may be recognized by a single hoof.

The only wonder is that Etna had not married, out of hand, this chivalric Chattanoogian, who selected consumptive little girls, whom even the scarlet fever and the measles spared, for victims—having first killed off their big brothers—who told over his adul teries as a monk might his beads, and as little blushed in telling them.

Seducing the sister, by way of getting even with her brother, certainly commends itself as an original enterprise, which should have stirred the depths of a refined and cultivated woman, emulous of elevating her kind by writing for the fashion magazines, to love and admiration. However, Etna declined the honor of a betrothal. It may have been that she was not ambitious of being set up as a target, etc., or wearing serge garments, etc., and early habits may have led her to object to even the remote possibility of being smothered with a pillow. At all events, she

11

said No, though she felt in her own heart that she loved him more than ever.

Oh, the feminine bosom! is it not fearfully and wonderfully made up!

Even the picture of the apple-trees, where he and his "idol had chatted, and romped, and whistled in in the far past" (think of that idle whistling!) failed to move her. She did not wish to incur the risk of having a "hemorrhage of *blood*," and besides, ambitious of authorship, she was determined to do it or die. It was a clear case of *noblesse oblige*.

CHAPTER X.

HE night mail brought her an offer of a situation as nurse in a rich but respectable family in New-York, and replies to her letters to the editors.

The Boston *Illuminati* wrote that they did not think that her style would do for the Atlantic—it was scarcely salt enough ; Philadelphia, speaking through Godey, replied that neither her essay on Ramayana, nor her very elaborate treatise on Comparative Anatomy was calculated to interest lady readers. They were declined with thanks—a polite editorial phrase· which may always be interpreted as meaning thanks that there is no more. The Harpers wanted practical articles that themselves and others could understand, without foot-notes, or condensations of their last published books, though they would publish extracts from her more serious essays in the Editor's Drawer, at the usual compensation in that department.

Seeing a gleam of hope here, Etna telegraphed to know what that rate was. The reply came, "Nothing, and pay your own postage."

But there was one ray of comfort. A new magazine had been started, and its proprietors were pushing it vigorously—so vigorously that they nearly pushed it to the wall in the first year of its existence. The public are not always in a milky and watery way, and sometimes crave something with an edge— meat-axy, rather than any other "axy." Hearing that the new magazine was then publishing some story by A trollop, Etna at first shrank sensitively back from such association, but finally made overtures of a glorious piece on favorable terms, inclosing to it an essay, "Who smote the marble brow of Billy Patterson?" In accordance with his usual custom the editor carried it home and read it to his wife, his father-in-law, his maid-servant, his man-servant, and the stranger that was within his gates. Not one of them being able to understand it, they unanimously voted it a delightful and excellent article, especially "maganizy," whatever that may mean; and Etna was informed that it would appear in the next number if another was issued. The editor added that it would be paid for at the regular rate, which was $1.10 a page.

At this latter clause Etna smiled a smile of love and triumph ; " For," she said, " there are forty pages, and I can buy a new dictionary for myself, of which I stand in need, and a New Testament for St. Twel'-mo, of which he stands in need, and also"—

But her countenance fell as she went on and read that they paid nothing for quotations, which would cut her article down to something less than three pages.

She sighed, and thought how hard it is to earn one's living by one's pen.

CHAPTER XI.

TNA went to New-York, and assumed her duties as nurse. It is recorded of her that she made a very dry nurse indeed.

Two children were entrusted to her care ; one a babe at the breast ; the other a precocious little fellow, with a weak back, named Felix.

The children made astonishing progress under her tuition. The baby spoke an unintelligible tongue before it was weaned, and Felix was well up in Hebrew before the first six months were ended. Felix, however, though very proud of the language, remarked that he didn't like the prayer of Habakkuk, or, as he pronounced it, "A back ache."

Her manner of instilling knowledge into the young mind was original and peculiar to herself. She encouraged them to ask questions which no one could answer, and never lost an opportunity of telling them something that they didn't know, and ought not to.

The system is known as "object teaching," I think. Thus to Felix one day, "No, my dear, the young oyster does not derive nourishment in the same way that your little brother does. The young oyster has a mamma, but the maternal oyster has no *mammæ.*"

"That is singular," cried Felix.

"No, my dear," replied Etna, "it is plural."

"This is a great deprivation," she continued, "but the meek resignation with which he submits to the dispensation, the patience with which he blindly fumbles about the rocks for his food, should teach little boys a lesson.

The parents of the children voted her a treasure, for she talked the children to sleep, and the paregoric and soothing-syrup account dwindled down to a merely nominal sum. In return, they allowed her to receive as many calls as she pleased, provided she herself answered the bell.

That her visits were not those of angels may be inferred from the number ; they were neither few nor far between. Her article in the magazine had sent all the Galactophagists to their dictionaries, and they could not find more than half the words there. In consequence, they came to Etna for elucidation, but she, unfortunately, had forgotten what the largest ones meant.   The effect of Etna's article was such that the magazine in which it appeared was afterwards published only once in two months instead of twice a month as at first, which was a vast improvement and delighted the public greatly.   All this won for Etna great reputation, and finally she had an offer to write for the *Ledger*.

Among the many who came to call, came an editor with a " granite mouth."

No, it was not Marble, nor yet the late Dr. Stone, and the reader need not indulge in conjectures as to what editor it may be.   It is quite enough to say that he wanted to marry Etna—a fact which at once establishes him as a man of determination and daring.

Etna refused him.   No one could guess why, for he owned a paper of his own, and was in a fair way of obtaining a foreign mission, as his party, then in power, had long been looking for a pretext to get him out of the country. When asked the reason of her refusing so eligible an offer, Etna replied it was his granite month; she did not like the formation.

Indeed, she had no end of offers.   An English lord, tall and handsome, with long side-whiskers and a double-barrelled eye-glass (it was *not* Lord Lyons), offered her marriage at sight.

It could scarcely be called a case of second sight, on her part, for she didn't see it.

She replied by reciting three chapters from the Gita-Govinda. " Great 'Evans ! " cried the lord, and took passage for England the next day. He will probably never return to this country, unless it be as a commissioner to settle the Alabama claims.

This thing must be kept up, thought Etna, and she next published a book. This made a hit—striking the publisher favorably, as he announced in a series of fantastic advertisments. Type of the most wonderful characters had to be cast expressly for the production of this work, and the services of the Learned Blacksmith were engaged as a chief proofreader — he should be kept well up in tongs, said Etna. Fifteen cylinder presses were kept running night and day to supply the demand, and the publisher was so broken down in health by the labor of writing advertisements, answering questions, and doing battle with the half-educated idiots who couldn't understand the book that he took in a partner and sailed himself for an uninhabited island to recuperate his shattered constitution. He had a good time on the island, and discovered some big things in ornithology.

In fact, never was there seen such a time. People came from all parts of the earth, including Boston, to see the authoress. She was photographed and photosculptured, and the dear dickens only knew what wasn't done to her; and everybody wanted to marry her, even little Felix, whom too much learning had made mad.

But Etna wouldn't marry any body, and finally sailed for England with the children, to get away from importunities, and it is said that she even turned longing eyes to Heaven—where it is popular· ly supposed that there is neither marriage nor giving in marriage—as a refuge.

In England every body wanted to marry her, and the yacht club gave her a dinner. In return she offered to present Prince Alfred with a copy of her book, which he respectfully declined, saying that he could not think of accepting any thing so valuable. She was even importuned to lecture in Exeter Hall paying the expenses of the building herself and guaranteeing that the furniture should not be demolished by the audience. This proposition she refused. But she consented to read an essay in private, upon the points of similarity between the Christian deities and heathen gods; the essay was spoken of by those who heard it as " a most exhaustive one"—indeed, it must have been, for nearly all who sat it through sank off to sleep.

Little Felix died. But Etna was somewhat consoled for the death of her charge by hearing of the " new birth" of her lover. The first dispatch—the Atlantic cable was not working very well then—spelt it berth, and stated that St. Twel'mo had been ordained as a circus rider. But a letter by the Cunard corrected the canard, and Etna learnt, to her great joy, that Circuit rider was meant, and her beloved was a minister.

At first she could not believe the news, but returning to Chattanooga, as soon as steam and rail could carry her, she found it confirmed. He had run through most of his property, people said, and no other profession was open to him.

The war breaking out just then, Etna determined that St. Twel'mo should not be at peace, and married him. She knew that the cause of the South was pure and just, and that they had a right to forts, arsenals, territory, and things that they had not paid for, and she was perfectly willing to sacrifice her best beloved to establish the sincerity of her convictions. Partly by her influence, but chiefly for

lack of any other material, he was made Bishop by
brevet, and Brigadier-General by confirmation. Unfortunately, for the cause which she knew to be
pure and just, his sermons bored his soldiers sadly,
while his generalship did not at all harass the enemy.
Had the Northern forces been obliged to face his
sermons instead of taking his positions, in all human
probability, the contest would have terminated differently.

As it was, however, the victorious armies swept
over and around Lookout Mountain, and surrender,
on the part of its defenders, became a Pantheistic
Necessity—the bear-garden was stripped naked, the
elephants, rhinoceroses, etc., having been killed and
eaten by the half-starved soldiery, in the first stages
of the siege. The Herring safe was carried off and
did duty for memorable months of the campaign as
a meat-safe at the headquarters of the invading army.
In short, if any one can find a trace of Le Beaucage
in the vicinity of Lookout Mountain, point to its
locality, or even bring forward a reliable gentleman
or intelligent contraband who ever saw it, he will be
rewarded handsomely. St. Twel'mo is shelved.

My story is done. I am not aware that it has any

moral, nor did I design any in the outset, beyond indicating the danger of leaving dictionaries in the way of children, and pointing that peculiarity in woman's nature which inspires them to love those who beat and bite them. However, if any can glean other morals from it, they are at perfect liberty so to do.

JOHN PAUL.

LESSONS IN BIOGRAPHY.

(An extract from the life of Dr. Pozz, in ten volumes, folio, written by James Bozz, Esq., who flourished with him near fifty years.)

By Rev. James Beresford.

E dined at the chop-house ; Dr. Pozz was this day very instructive. Talking of books, I mentioned the "*History of Tommy Trip*, and said it was a great work." *Pozz.* —"Yes, sir, it is great, relatively; it was a great work to you when you were a little boy ; but now, sir, you are a great man, and Tommy Trip is a little man."

Feeling somewhat hurt at this comparison,—I believe he perceived it, for as he was squeezing a lemon, he said,—"Never be affronted at a comparison ; I have been compared to many things, yet I never was affronted at a comparison. No, sir, if they were to call me a dog, and you a canister tied to my tail, I should not be affronted."

Cheered by this kind mention of me, though in *such* company, I asked him what he thought of a friend of ours who was always making comparisons. *Pozz.*—" Sir, that fellow has a simile for everything. I knew him when he kept shop,—he then made money, and now he makes comparisons ; he would say, for instance, that you and I were two figs stuck together, two figs in adhesion, and then he would laugh."

To this vivid exertion of intellect, I observed in reply, " Certain great writers have determined that comparisons are odious." *Pozz.* " No, sir, not odious as comparisons. The fellows who make them are odious ; the whigs make comparisons."

We supped that evening at his house, when I took an opportunity of showing him a copy of verses I had made on a pair of breeches. *Pozz.*—" Sir, the lines are good ; but where do you find such a subject in Scotland ? *Bozz.*—" The greater the proof of invention, which is a characteristic of Poetry." *Pozz.*— " Yes, sir, but it is an invention which few of your countrymen can enjoy." I reflected afterwards on the depth of this remark. It affords a proof of that profundity which he displays in every branch of literature.

Having accidentally asked him if he approved of green spectacles, he made answer : "As to green spectacles, sir, the question seems to be this,—if I wore green spectacles, it would be because they assisted vision, or because I liked them ; but if a man were to tell me he did not like green spectacles, and that they hurt his eyes, I do not compel him to wear them. No, sir, I would rather dissuade him from making use of them."

A few months after, I consulted him again on this subject, and he honored me with a letter, in which he confirmed his former opinion : it may be found in the proper place, vol vi. page 2789. And having since that time maturely considered the point myself, I must needs confess, that in all such matters, a man ought to be a free moral agent.

The next day I left town for six weeks, three days and seven hours, as I find by a memorandum in my Journal. During this time I received only one letter from him, which is as follows :

"To James Bozz, Esq.

   "Dear Sir,"

   " My bowels have been very bad ; Pray buy for me

some Turkey rhubarb, and bring with you a copy of your tour. Write me soon, and write me often.

" I am, dear sir,

" Yours affectionately,

" SAM. POZZ."

It would have been unpardonable to have omitted a letter in which we see so much of his great and illuminated mind.

On my return to town, we met again at the chop-house, and had a long as well as a highly interesting conversation; indeed, there is not one hour of my life in which I do not profit by some part of his valuable communications.

On medical subjects his knowledge was immense. He told me that one of our friends had just been attacked by an alarming complaint. He had entirely lost the use of his limbs,—he was speechless,— his eyes swollen, and every vein distended; yet his face was pale, and his extremities cold, at the same time his pulse beat one hundred and sixty strokes in a minute.

I said, with tenderness, that I would immediately go and see him, and take Dr. Bolus with me. *Pozz.*— " No, sir, don't go." I was startled at so unexpected a reply, well knowing his compassionate heart, and

12

earnestly demanded of him the reason why I should not procure for the afflicted person instant relief. *Pozz.*—" Sir, you do not know his disorder." *Bozz.* —" Pray what is it ? " *Pozz.*—" Sir, the man is *dead drunk.*"

This explanation threw me into a violent fit of laughter, in which he joined me, rolling about as he used to do when he enjoyed a joke ; but he afterwards checked me, by the following words : " Sir, you ought not to laugh at what I said, for he who laughs at what another man says, will soon laugh at that other man. Sir, you ought to laugh but seldom. You ought to laugh only at your own jokes."

Talking of a friend of ours, who was a very violent politician, I said " I did not like his company." *Pozz.*—" No, sir, he is not healthy, he is sore. Sir, his mind is ulcerated,—he has a political whitlow ; you cannot touch him, sir, without giving him pain. I would never venture to speak on political subjects with that man ; I would talk of cabbage and of peas. Sir, I would ask him how he got his corn in, but I would not meddle with politics." *Bozz.*—" But perhaps, sir, he would talk of nothing else." *Pozz.* —" Then it is plain what he would do." On my earnestly entreating him to tell me what that was, Dr.

Bozz replied : " Sir, he would let everything else alone."

I mentioned a tradesman who had lately set up a coach. *Pozz.*—" You are right, sir, a man who would go on swimmingly cannot be too soon off his legs. You tell me he keeps a coach ; now, sir, a coach is better than a chaise ; sir, it is better than a chariot." *Bozz.*—" Why, sir ?" *Pozz.*—" It will hold more." I begged he would repeat this valuable observation, in order to impress it on my memory, and he complied with great good-humor.

Taking a hint from the subject of our present conversation, I said : " Dr. Pozz, *you* ought to keep a coach." *Pozz.*—" Yes, sir, I ought." *Bozz.*—" But you do not, and this has often surprised me." *Pozz.* —" Surprised you ! There, sir, is another prejudice of absurdity. Sir, you ought to be surprised at nothing ; a man who has lived half so long as you, ought to be above surprise. It is a rule with me, sir, never to be surprised."

" This is an error," continued Dr. Pozz, " produced by ignorance ; you cannot guess why I do not keep a coach, and you are surprised ! now sir, if you did know, you would not be surprised." I said tenderly, " I hope, my dear sir, you will let me know before I leave town." *Pozz.*—"Yes, sir, you shall now know ; the reason why I do not keep a coach is, because I can't afford it."

We talked of drinking ; I asked him whether, in the course of his long and valuable life, he had not known some men who drank more than they could bear. *Pozz.*—"Yes, sir, and then nobody could bear them ; a man who is drunk, sir, is a very foolish fellow. *Bozz.*—But, sir, as the poet says, he is devoid of all care." *Pozz.*—"That is true, sir, he cares for nobody ; he has none of the cares of life ; he cannot be a merchant, sir, for he is unable to write his name ; he cannot be a politician, sir, for he is almost speechless ; he cannot be an artist, sir, for he is nearly blind ; and yet, sir, there is a science in drinking." *Bozz.*—"I suppose you mean that a man ought to know what he drinks." *Pozz.*—No, sir, to know what one drinks is nothing, but the science consists of three parts ; in knowing when we have had too little, when we have had too much, and when we have had enough. For instance, there is our friend * * * *, he can always tell when he has too little, and when he has too much, but never knows when he has enough."

We talked this day on a variety of subjects, but I

find few memorandums in my journal; on small beer, he said it was a flatulent liquor   He disapproved of those who deny the utility of absolute power, and seemed to be offended with a friend of ours who would always have his eggs poached. Sign posts, he observed, had very much degenerated within his memory, and he found great fault with the moral of the Beggar's Opera.

I endeavored to defend a play which had afforded me so much pleasure, but could not muster that strength of mind with which he argued; and it was with great satisfaction that he afterwards communicated to me a method of curing corns by the application of a piece of oiled silk.   In the early history of the world he preferred Sir Isaac Newton to chronology; but as they gave employment to so many hands, he did not dislike the large shoe-buckles then in the fashion.

Next day we dined at the Mitre; I mentioned spirits. *Pozz.*—" Sir, there is as much evidence for the existence of spirits as against it ; you may not believe it ; but you cannot deny it." I told him that my great grandmother once saw a spirit ; he desired me to relate the circumstances, which I did very minutely, while he listened with profound attention.

When I mentioned that the spirit once appeared in the shape of a shoulder of mutton, and another time in that of a tea-pot, he interrupted me. *Pozz.*— "There, sir, is the point, the evidence is good, but the scheme is defective in consistency; we cannot deny that the spirits appeared in these shapes; but then we cannot reconcile them; for what has a teapot to do with a shoulder of mutton? The objects, sir, are neither terrific nor contemporaneous; they are never seen at the same time, nor in the same place." *Pozz.*— "I think, sir, that ghosts are most often seen by old women." *Pozz.*— "Yes, sir, and their conversation is generally full of the subject; I would prefer old women to record such circumstances, their loquacity tends to minuteness."

A few days after this interesting and enlightened conversation, we talked of a person who had a very bad character. *Pozz.*— "Sir, he is a scoundrel." *Bozz.*— "I hate a scoundrel." *Pozz.*— "There you are wrong; I would not have you hate scoundrels; scoundrels, sir, are useful; there are many things we cannot do without scoundrels. I should not choose to keep company with scoundrels; neither would I introduce them to my wife and children; but something may be got from them." *Bozz.*— "Are not scoundrels for the most part fools?" *Pozz.*—"No sir, they are not. A scoundrel must be a clever fellow ; he must know many things of which a fool is ignorant. Any man may be a fool, but to be a complete rascal, requires considerable abilities. I think a good book might be written on the subject of scoundrels : a *Biographia Flagitiosa*, or the lives of eminent scoundrels, from the earliest accounts to the present time."

Hanging was mentioned in the course of the conversation, and I observed that it was a very awkward situation. *Pozz.*—"No, sir, hanging is not an awkward situation ; it is proper, sir, that a man whose actions tend to flagitious obliquity should himself be perpendicular."

I told Doctor Pozz, that I had lately been in company with a number of gentlemen, all of whom could recollect some friend or other who had been hanged. *Pozz.*—"Yes, sir, we know those who *have* been hanged,—that is a circumstance we can easily recollect, and may safely mention, without fear of offence, but we must not name those who *deserve* it— such a proceeding would not be decorous in good company ; it is one of those things we may *think* but must not speak of.

JOHN JENKINS;

OR

THE SMOKER REFORMED.

By T. S. A—TH—R.

CHAPTER I.

NE cigar a day!" said Judge Boompointer. "One cigar a day!" repeated John Jenkins, as with trepidation he dropped his half-consumed cigar under his work-bench.

"One cigar a day is three cents a day," remarked Judge Boompointer, gravely; "and do you know, sir, what one cigar a day, or three cents a day, amounts to in the course of four years?"

John Jenkins, in his boyhood, had attended the village school, and possessed considerable arithmetical ability. Taking up a shingle which lay upon his work-bench, and producing a piece of chalk, with a feeling of conscious pride he made an exhaustive calculation.

" Exactly forty-three dollars and eighty cents," he replied, wiping the perspiration from his heated brow, while his face flushed with honest enthusiasm.

" Well, sir, if you saved three cents a day, instead of wasting it, you would now be the possessor of a new suit of clothes, an illustrated Family Bible, a pew in the church, a complete set of Patent Office Reports, a hymn-book, and a paid subscription to *Authur's Home Magazine*, which could be purchased for exactly forty-three dollars and eighty cents ; and," added the Judge, with increasing sternness, " if you calculate leap-year, which you seem to have strangely omitted, you have three cents more, sir ; *three cents more !* What would that buy you, sir ? "

" A cigar," suggested John Jenkins ; but, coloring again deeply, he hid his face.

" No, sir," said the Judge, with a sweet smile of benevolence stealing over his stern features ; "properly invested, it would buy you that which passeth all price. Dropped into the missionary-box, who can tell what heathen, now idly and joyously wanton-

ing in nakedness and sin, might be brought to a
sense of his miserable condition, and made, through
that three cents, to feel the torments of the wicked?"

With these words the Judge retired, leaving John
Jenkins buried in profound thought. " Three cents
a day," he muttered. " In forty years I might be
worth four hundred and thirty-eight dollars and ten
cents,—and then I might marry Mary. Ah, Mary!"
The young carpenter sighed, and, drawing a twenty-
five cent daguerreotype from his vest-pocket, gazed
long and fervidly upon the features of a young girl
in book muslin and a coral necklace. Then, with
a resolute expression, he carefully locked the door
of his workshop and departed.

Alas! his good resolutions were too late. We
trifle with the tide of fortune which too often nips
us in the bud and casts the dark shadow of misfortune over the bright lexicon of youth! That night
the half-consumed fragment of John Jenkins's cigar
set fire to his workshop and burned it up, together
with all his tools and materials. There was no
insurance.

CHAPTER II.

HEN you still persist in marrying John Jenkins?" queried Judge Boompointer as he playfully, with paternal familiarity, lifted the golden curls of the village belle, Mary Jones.

"I do," replied the fair young girl, in a low voice, that resembled rock candy in its saccharine firmness,—"I do. He has promised to reform. Since he lost all his property by fire — "

"The result of his pernicious habit, though he illogically persists in charging it to me," interrupted the Judge.

"Since then," continued the young girl, " he has endeavored to break himself of the habit. He tells me that he has substituted the stalks of the Indian ratan, the outer part of a leguminous plant called

the smoking-bean, and the fragmentary and uncon-
sumed remainder of cigars which occur at rare and
uncertain intervals along the road, which, as he in-
forms me, though deficient in quality and strength,
are comparatively inexpensive." And, blushing at
her own eloquence, the young girl hid her curls on
the Judge's arm.

"Poor thing!" muttered Judge Boompointer.
"Dare I tell her all? Yet I must." ˈ

"I shall cling to him," continued the young girl
rising with her theme, "as the young vine clings
to some hoary ruin. Nay, nay, chide me not, Judge
Boompointer. I will marry John Jenkins!"

The Judge was evidently affected. Seating himself at the table, he wrote a few lines hurriedly upon
a piece of paper, which he folded and placed in the
fingers of the destined bride of John Jenkins.

"Mary Jones," said the Judge, with impressive
earnestness, "take this trifle as a wedding gift from
one who respects your fidelity and truthfulness.
At the altar let it be a reminder of me." And cov-
ering his face hastily with a handkerchief, the stern
and iron-willed man left the room. As the door
closed, Mary unfolded the paper. It was an order
on the corner grocery for three yards of flannel, a

paper of needles, four pounds of soap, one pound of starch, and two boxes of matches!

"Noble and thoughtful man!" was all Mary Jones could exclaim, as she hid her face in her hands and burst into a flood of tears.

*   *   *   *   *

The bells of Cloverdale are ringing merrily. It is a wedding. "How beautiful they look!" is the exclamation that passes from lip to lip, as Mary Jones, leaning timidly on the arm of John Jenkins, enters the church. But the bride is agitated, and the bridegroom betrays a feverish nervousness. As they stand in the vestibule, John Jenkins fumbles earnestly in his vest-pocket. Can it be the ring he is anxious about? No. He draws a small brown substance from his pocket, and biting off a piece, hastily replaces the fragment and gazes furtively around. Surely no one saw him? Alas! the eyes of two of that wedding party saw the fatal act. Judge Boompointer shook his head sternly. Mary Jones sighed and breathed a silent prayer. Her husband chewed!

HAT! more bread?" said John Jenkins gruffly. "You're always asking for money for bread. D—nation! Do you want to ruin me by your extravagance?" and as he uttered these words he drew from his pocket a bottle of whiskey, a pipe, and a paper of tobacco. Emptying the first at a draught, he threw the empty bottle at the head of his eldest boy, a youth of twelve summers. The missile stuck the child full in the temple, and stretched him a lifeless corpse. Mrs. Jenkins, whom the reader will hardly recognize as the once gay and beautiful Mary Jones, raised the dead body of her son in her arms, and carefully placing the unfortunate youth beside the pump in the back yard, returned with saddened step to the house. At another time, and in brighter days, she might have wept at the occurrence. She was past tears now.

" Father, your conduct is reprehensible ! " said little Harrison Jenkins, the youngest boy. " Where do you expect to go when you die ? "

" Ah ! " said John Jenkins, fiercely ; " this comes of giving children a liberal education ; this is the result of Sabbath schools. Down, viper ! "

A tumbler thrown from the same parental fist laid out the youthful Harrison cold. The four other children had, in the mean time, gathered around the table with anxious expectancy. With a chuckle, the now changed and brutal John Jenkins produced four pipes, and, filling them with tobacco, handed one to each of his offspring and bade them smoke. " It's better than bread ! " laughed the wretch, hoarsely.

Mary Jenkins though of a patient nature, felt it her duty now to speak. " I have borne much, John Jenkins," she said. " But I prefer that the children should not smoke. It is an unclean habit, and soils their clothes. I ask this as a special favor ! "

John Jenkins hesitated,—the pangs of remorse began to seize him.

" Promise me this, John ! " urged Mary upon her knees.

" I promise ! " reluctantly answered John.

" And you will put the money in a savings-bank ?"

" I will," repeated her husband ; " and I'll give up smoking, too."

" 'T is well, John Jenkins!" said Judge Boompointer, appearing suddenly from behind the door, where he had been concealed during this interview. " Nobly said ! my man. Cheer up ! I will see that the children are decently buried." The husband and wife fell into each other's arms. And Judge Boompointer, gazing upon the affecting spectacle, burst into tears.

From that day John Jenkins was an altered man.

BRET HARTE.

IIO-FI OF TIIE YELLOW GIRDLE.

Adapted from the Chinese of Hou-de-Kaw-Lim.[*]

BY T. T. T.

ORE graceful than the bamboo, and fairer than rice, was So-Sli, the daughter of the philosopher Poo-Poo. Her foot was no longer than her finger; so that, when she walked, she tottered in the most engaging manner, and was obliged to seek the support of a reed or of a hand-maiden. So light was her form, and so lovely was her face, and so helpless was her air, that, when she

[*] A writer as prolific and various as our own Anon. Ile resembles that writer, too, in the ill-fortune which has militated against his obtaining the fame due to his genius and industry, from the authorship of all his most excellent works having been uniformly claimed by unprincipled and shameless persons, who have succeeded in tearing the bamboo-sprigs from his brows. Ile is still living, though arrived at a patriarchal age. No library can be considered complete without a collected edition of his works. — T. T. T.

appeared abroad, she attracted the notice of all, as a straw which a juggler of Shanghai balances on the tip of his nose. Her brows were arched like the feathers in the tail of the domestic bird of the river; her eyes were smaller than the kernels of the almond, and were free from the disfigurement of lashes; her hair was like a cobweb of the black spiders of Chensi; her nose was small and beautifully flat; her lips were as two large pink caterpillars, which the cooks of Pecheli have prepared in the banquet for the Son of Heaven. The fame of her loveliness had spread through the province Kiang-Si; and many a manly spirit yearned towards her, even upon the *report* of her beauty.

Many were the solicitations made to her father for the hand of the lovely So-Sli; and he might have married her to mandarins, both civil and military, as many as he. pleased. But old Poo-Poo was a sage and a philanthropist, and had devoted himself much to the investigation of causes of human happiness and misery, and had determined that marriage might be highly conducive to one or to the other, according as it should be, or should not be, conducted upon scientific principles. Of the scientific principles upon which marriage should be conducted, he had formed a theory of his own; and it had been a source of the deepest regret to him, that he had not devised his theory until after his own marriage.

However, as his wife was now dead, that had become a matter of comparatively little importance. He determined that his daughter should have the full benefit to be derived from his idea; and, for a Chinese, it must be conceded that his principles exhibited much liberality of feeling. This was particularly evinced in one of his theorems, — a theorem which, however, appeared in the eyes of his countrymen so extraordinary, that, but for some charitable doubts which were entertained as to his sanity, it would probably have brought down upon him the heavy displeasure of the government.

He was the first of the Celestial people who had ever questioned or doubted the propriety of a marriage between persons who had had no previous acquaintance with each other. He was rash enough to start and maintain this opinion; and, further-more, he considered that a certain somewhat of congeniality should subsist between, and be dis-covered by, the parties, before they should proceed to bind themselves indissolubly together. He determined, therefore, not only that his daughter should see her future lord before she became a wife, but such was the peculiar tenderness of his paternal affection, and so far had the heresy of innovation possessed him, that she should not be made over to any person towards whom she manifested a decided dislike.

Two great mandarins, Hang-Yu and Yu-be-Hung, and a certain rich merchant, Tin, had sent costly presents to her father; and the eloquent Tung, a graduate of the college of Hanlan, had composed ten volumes of moral sentences in praise of the beauty of So-Sli: but though he perused the books, and graciously accepted the presents, Poo-Poo rejected these applicants, who lived too far off to make their addresses in person. It fared no better with many of various rank, — manufacturers, and proprietors of rice-grounds, silk-feeders, barge-owners, and officers, civil and military, who, dwelling in the neighborhood, had opportunities of seeing, and of being looked upon by, the lovely eyes of So-Sli. She had expressed herself as being by no means averse to Tung, or to Tin, to Hang-Yu, or Yu-be-Hung; but these she had never seen. Those whom she saw found no favor in her sight. One

was too tall ; another was too short ; a third was too
fat ; a fourth too thin ; this too gay ; and that too
serious. Ting-a-Ting's voice was too gentle : Ding-
Dong's was too loud. One was too fond of sweet-
potato, and sweet-potato she disliked : another, not
sufficiently partial to dog, and dog was her favorite
dish. In fact, So-Sli was by no means easy to
please.

Here we may pause to remark, that the multi-
plicity of presents which for a long time poured in
upon Poo-Poo were well-nigh procuring converts to
his system among old gentlemen who had marriage-
able daughters ; but at last suitors grew chary of
their presents, and withheld them till an interview
with the young lady should have sealed their
fortune.

In the town in which dwelt Poo-Poo and his
lovely daughter So-Sli, there resided a young man
who boasted his relationship to the imperial family,
being, in fact, a descendant from an emperor who
had occupied the throne about a hundred and fifty
years before.

The Emperor of China looks with commendable
affection upon all his poor relations, of whom he
keeps an inventory of about ten thousand ; and,

according to their several degrees of affinity, he allots to all, by a graduated scale, certain annual stipends, and permits them to wear some badge by which they may be distinguished as being of his kin. This badge, whether cloak, or shawl, or belt, or cap, is of the imperial color, yellow; and in the particular instance of Ho-Fi, the young man of whom we speak, was a silken girdle, whence he was known throughout that neighborhood as Ho-Fi of the Yellow Girdle. He furthermore enjoyed an allowance of three dollars, and two sacks of rice per month.

Being thus a cousin, though a distant one, of the Son of Heaven, he would have considered it much beneath his dignity to have followed for his livelihood any profession or trade; and, as he had desires and ambition to which his means were quite inadequate, he was driven to curious shifts, at times, in the vulgar words of the west, to procure salt for his porridge, or, indeed, porridge for his salt.

Ho-Fi heard all the tongues of the neighborhood eloquent in praise of the beauty of So-Sli; but he heard them, likewise, no less voluble in condemnation of her whimsicality and waywardness. Fresh stories were every day told of her rejection of some meritorious suitor; and, as none seemed likely to prove altogether agreeable to her very fastidious taste, those who would have been glad to obtain such a prize became shy of advancing their claims. But Ho-Fi, with less intrinsic worth than many, was not of a character to be daunted by the fear of the negotiation proving unsatisfactory; and he resolved to enlist himself as one of the competitors for the hand of So-Sli.

Ho-Fi, though quite a young man, had already been six times married, and on every occasion had had the misfortune to lose his wife within a few weeks after their union. As seven is accounted a particularly fortunate number, it is not to be wondered at that he was desirous to adventure once more. His six dear wives were all laid on the shelf together; and he wanted one other in order " to make up a set."

Ho-Fi rejoiced in many advantages which had already several times stood him in good stead in circumstances somewhat similar to those in which he was about to exert his tactics. He was possessed of what his lovely countrywomen were prone to consider a handsome person. His finger-nails, by virtue of well-contrived splints, he managed to

maintain an inch and a half in length; he was
quite free from whiskers or beard; and his head was
always kept cleanly shaven, except the usual tuft at
the crown, which, of peculiar blackness and strength,
and neatly tied up with silk, depended down his
back almost to the bend of his knee. He was particular, moreover, in his dress; and, as it was well
known that his funds were of the most limited, it
was a matter of surprise among his neighbors how
he became possessed of so very respectable a ward-
robe. And, if this was a mystery to them, what
wonder that I, a stranger and barbarian, am quite
unable to explain it? I leave it to your conjectures,
and I feel sure that there are some among my
countrymen to whom a solution will be intuitively
easy. Person and dress, it will be admitted, serve
as two powerful talismans in such adventures as that
upon which he was going to set forth; but he was
possessed of other advantages incalculably more
important. These were a limitless assurance, and
that determined perseverance, which, disregarding
repulses, returns again and again to the charge;
or which in simpler phrase, will not take *no* for an
answer. To these may be added an adaptability of
disposition, which could fall in with the humors of

all parties, and a readiness in discovering the weak
points of the enemy, and directing an attack accordingly.

" 'Tis but venturing," said Ho-Fi ; " and, if I fail,
I will not hang myself up by my pig-tail, like a Boo-
Bee, nor run myself through with a thumb-nail, like
a Ni-Ni." Boo-Bee and Ni-Ni were two celebrated
Werters of China.

His design thus formed, he set systematically to
work to carry it into effect, and began by picking
acquaintance with the philosopher Poo-Poo. Observing that venerable person cheapening the hind-
quarter of a prize pole-cat in the meat-market, with
his usual ease and address he managed to fall into
conversation with him ; and by a little banter, from
time to time, agreeably directed to the butcher, soon
obtained for the philosopher that abatement in the
price of the tempting morsel, for which Poo-Poo
himself might, probably, in vain have striven. Having declared his own predilection for pole-cat, and
particularly for the hind-quarter, he led the discourse by easy gradations from pole-cats to weasels,
from weasels to rats, from rats to dogs, from dogs to
pigs, from pigs to his fair countrywomen, and so to
the celebrated beauty So-Sli, the daughter of the

sage Poo-Poo. Of the philosopher himself he expressed great admiration, and regretted that he was not so fortunate as to enjoy his acquaintance, nay, that he did not even so much as know him by sight. Poo-Poo was a lover of wisdom; but what philosopher was ever yet proof against adulation? or would not feel gratified at overhearing his own praises in cases like the present, where they could not be intended as flattery? Ho-Fi had already secured himself a high place in the philosophical estimation of Poo-Poo.

It will readily be supposed that Poo-Poo was not anxious to turn the conversation out of the channel into which it had thus accidentally flowed; and he sounded his new friend's opinions on the subject of his pet matrimonial theory. This Ho-Fi of course applauded "to the very echo," by which expression is intended that his words were mere mockery, *vox et pretereu nihil.*

"Were you to ask me," said he, "who is the greatest of ancient or modern sages, I should answer, Poo-Poo. Were you to ask me, who, of all, has advanced a theory most likly to be extensively beneficial to the human race, I should answer, Poo-Poo. Nor do I doubt but that the day will come when the wisdom of Poo-Poo will be universally admitted, and his name be adduced as a conclusive settlement of all disputed questions; when, if any one shall be asked his reason, he will answer, Poo-Poo; if he be asked his authority, he will answer, Poo-Poo; when criticism will be condensed in those two syllables, Poo-Poo; and when those same two syllables, Poo-Poo, will suffice to upset criticism; in short, when he that speaks Poo-Poo the loudest will be the best logician, and when all discussion will be but a matter of Poo-Poo."

That day Ho-Fi dined with Poo-Poo on the hind-quarter of the prize pole-cat.

The morsel was small, but it was choice.

Having so soon and so easily insinuated himself into the good graces of the father, he next sought an opportunity of winning his way into those of the daughter. He boldly expressed his desire to Poo-Poo; and a day was settled upon which he should be formally introduced to her, — a ceremony not to be conducted with too great precipitation. In the interval, he was careful to collect all information regarding the whims and prejudices of the lovely So-Sli.

He came, he saw. he conquered; or, we should

rather write, he came, *she* saw, he conquered. His attire was studiously elegant ; and he had selected such colors as he had found, from the report of some of her acquaintance, were the most agreeable to her. His beautifully-embroidered petticoat of crimson silk was well calculated to take the feminine fancy ; his shawl might have won the heart even of an English lady ; his cap he had procured from one of the most eminent *modistes* of Pekin ; and the tippet, which formed part of out-door dress, was of the most costly fur. His long black hair was carefully plaited, and hung far down his back ; he wore a necklace of pearls, much coveted by his young competitors in fashion ; his scent-bottle was replenished with the choicest essence ; and he carried a valuable fan, which he flourished with peculiar grace.

This attention to externals produced at once a favorable impression upon So-Sli, who was herself particular in her attire. She usually wore a long frock-coat of blue or green cloth over a pink waist-coat ; and her trousers were always of the newest cut. She went to considerable expense to procure the most elegant pipes, and piqued herself upon her nice judgment in her choice of tobacco.

The town, like some other Chinese towns, was

upon the point of surrendering to the formidable "demonstration" made by the enemy; but when he opened upon it simultaneously the light artillery of flattery and the heavy artillery of gifts (the latter consisting of two great guns, — the one a gold snuff-box, and the other a Chinese poodle), the gates flew open, and he marched in triumph into the citadel, — his lady's heart. The vanquished So-Sli kept the snuff-box, ate the poodle, and accepted the heart and the hand of Ho-Fi.

They were married, and a fortnight flew by in two days; or, perhaps, the young pair made some miscalculation, as the almanacs had not predicted this.

The cranium, we would observe, is the dwelling-house of the soul; the organ of time is its time-piece: but, when the soul sits all day in its back-rooms, it sometimes forgets to wind up its clock.

Each was constantly devising means to gratify the other; and the only occasions of strife that arose between them were when each endeavored to force upon the other the choicest morsels of fox, or ferret, or frog, or whatever constituted their delicate little meal for the day.

One morning Ho-Fi for a while absented himself from his beloved So-Sli, and went into the city.

When he returned, he took from his pouch, or reti-
cule, a small packet of tea.

"My dearest So-Sli," he said, "I have a friend
who is particular in the cultivation of plants. With
so much skill and care are his experiments conducted, that he has succeeded in obtaining bananas
from his orange-trees, and in converting a pine-apple
into a gooseberry. He has lately directed his attention to the improvement of a young tea-tree. He
planted it with a silver spade, manured it with silkworms and doves' marrow, and he daily waters the
earth around it with roe's teeth and cinnamon-juice.
He has hitherto gathered but two ounces of the
leaves, one of which has been presented to the emperor; and the other he has transmitted to me, as
being the oldest of his friends. So I have brought
it here for my darling So-Sli. As you love me,
make an infusion of its leaves, and drink."

"Nay," said So-Sli, "if it be so choice, you shall
drink it, not I. What exceedingly curious leaves!
And what is most remarkable about them is, that
they are exactly like others. But what is this dust
upon them?"

"That," answered Ho-Fi, "is a substance derived
from the silkworms, and is what, had they not been

buried, would have formed the down on the wings when they became moths. But you must drink this most dainty infusion : I have prepared it purposely for you ; and to refuse it would be to show how little you loved your tender Ho-Fi."

Whilst speaking, Ho-Fi had poured hot water on the leaves ; and he offered to his beloved the cup containing the fragrant infusion. She, however, insisted that he should drink it ; and an affectionate contest took place between them, each wishing to give up to the other all the enjoyment of so exquisite a draught. So-Sli at first positively refused to taste a drop ; then she would consent that he should leave one sip for her ; and then, that, if he would take half, she would drink the remainder. But Ho-Fi was obstinately determined that she should have all, or at least should take the first draught. At last their affectionate entreaties began to change to tones of anger and impatience ; when, to settle the matter at once, So-Sli took the cup, and, proceeding to the open window, emptied it in her husband's view, declaring, that, as it had become a cause of quarrel, it should not be tasted by either.

Their anger blew over, and several times since they had taken tea together in perfect amity. One

evening they were seated to that important occupation, and Ho-Fi had just finished his first cup, when
So-Sli observed she did not think the tea so good as
usual.　Ho-Fi agreed with her in opinion, and,
using a common Chinese imprecation, wished a rot-
ten root to the tree that bore it.

"What!" said So-Sli, bursting into a fit of uncon-
trollable laughter, "after all the pains your poor
friend has taken to nourish it with silkworms and
spice?　Oh! now that is too cruel a desire!"

Ho-Fi stared, and turned somewhat pale.

"Why do you revert to that subject?" he said.
"Methinks it were better to let such a matter rest."

"Nay," said So-Sli, still laughing violently, "I
said you should drink the tea; and, when I pretended
to pour it from the window, I poured it only into an
earthen pan which lay outside. I have had it
warmed for you now, but am sorry you like it so
little."

Ho-Fi turned very pale; and his pigtail, with the
effect of fear, stood out horizontally and stiffly from
his head.　For a few moments he was struck mo-
tionless; but anon he started up, and called loudly
for warm water.

"Perfidious woman!" he shrieked, "hast thou
poisoned thy husband?"

"Poisoned !" said So-Sli. "Was the tea then poisoned ? I remember that white dust; but can moths' feathers poison ? "

"It burns; it burns !" cried Ho-Fi in a frantic manner. "For Fo's sake bring me an emetic, a' stomach-pump — no, no, that is not yet invented — but blisters, cataplasms, any thing !"

He was put in bed ; physicians were sent for ; he raved till he was exhausted, and then lay asleep, or insensible, for some hours. When his sense returned, he became aware of the expressions he had used ; and, being calmer, he endeavored to explain them away. He said that the tea was of such wonderful potency as to have deprived him of reason more rapidly than the strong spirit distilled from rice could have done. He had fancied, in his delirium, that his wife had put poison in his cup ; but he now fully appreciated the absurdity of such a fear. He should write to the friend from whom he had received the leaves, a timely intimation, that, should the emperor swallow the infusion intended for the bodily solace of that Celestial person, he, the unfortunate cultivator of this ardent tea, would unquestionably be put to death by all the ingenuities of torture

14

Ho-Fi had a strong constitution to support him against poisoned tea and three Chinese physicians. He slowly recovered from their *effects*.

He was restored once more to his fond wife; but, fond as she had always shown herself, So-Sli could not prevent the intrusion into her mind of an unpleasant suspicion that her affectionate husband had offered her poisoned tea from a too lively solicitude to put her quite out of reach of those ugly customers, care and sorrow. Long before her marriage, surmises had been whispered, which had even reached her ears, that at least a few of his former six wives had been dealt with unfairly; but no one, wife or otherwise, volunteered any evidence against him; and the Chinese had not arrived at those refinements in chemical science, which enable our western luminaries, by distilling a bone, or making a fricassee of a muscle, to detect the millionth part of the shadow of nothing in one who is supposed to have died by poison.

It could hardly have been hinted that a man was such a Bluebeard, without strong reason assigned for so supposing. Perhaps, to some minds, the mere fact of his having been married six times, and having, in every instance, become a widower within two

months, may suffice to justify a suspicion; but, if
a *motive* should be sought that could render such
heinous villany probable, it might be mentioned,
that, on the marriage of a Yellow Girdle, he is
allowed by his cousin, the emperor, a sum of one
hundred taels (in addition to his usual stipend) to
assist in furnishing his house; and, on the death of
his wife, one hundred and twenty more, to assist in
furnishing her sepulchre. And Ho-Fi was by no
means the first of whom it had been reported that
he had sought, by a succession of such profitable
marriages and deaths, to raise his very inconsidera-
ble income into a handsome competency.

So-Sli could not avoid a suspicion; but, as she
had really loved Ho-Fi, she tried to repress it, and
not to entertain such evil thoughts as must, if confirmed, have given a death-blow to her affection.
Still she was haunted by a fear that he might
endeavor by other devices to lay her on the shelf
with his former wives. The "shelf" whereupon his
former wives were laid was a shelf of rock at a
small distance from the city, — a place upon which
such persons as could not afford to purchase ground
for the burial of their deceased friends, availed
themselves of the common right of disposing coffins.

He had, therefore, appropriated to himself a portion of this ledge, where the six coffins of his wives were ranged side by side, in the neatest order, like so many volumes of one book, that might, not inappropriately, have been termed collectively, " The Works of Ho-Fi." Upon each was inscribed the words, "Wife of Ho-Fi," and the name, besides, of the occupant as a brief table of contents.

I am sorry to say, that, had So-Sli been more suspicious than she was, she would therein have done her husband no wrong. There was nothing he so earnestly wished as to have his new volume firmly put up in a camphor-wood binding, and neatly lettered to match the others.

Ho-Fi remembered an incident in a famous Chinese tragedy, an original device for disposing of an obnoxious person, which he imagined he might turn to felicitous account. He procured a savage dog, and having purchased a lady's dress of peculiar colors, and another of similar appearance, although of inferior quality, he filled the latter with straw, bones, and offal, and encouraged the fierce animal to tear this effigy in pieces. The creature was well pleased with the prize he discovered within; and Ho-Fi repeated his experiments on several succes

sive days. When he considered the dog to be sufficiently familiarized with the figure, he tied him up,
and kept him for some time without food. The
insidious Yellow Girdle then made a present to his
lady of the other and choicer dress, expressing a
desire that she might immediately indue it. This,
not, however, until she had examined it with an
apprehensive eye, she did; and he affected to be
much gratified at beholding her in her new garment.
He, however, pretended to have business which
would call him from home for an hour, and begged
that she would wait his return in a grotto in the
garden; but he particularly requested that she
would allow no one to open a chest which he had
had placed in a court of the house, and of which
he said the fastening had been accidentally broken.
Excusing himself from explaining to her just then
what it contained, he promised that he would do
so by and by.

When So-Sli was left alone, she communed with
herself. " Who knows," she said, " what man-trap
or spring gun my beloved husband may have prepared for me in the grotto ? " It will not, I fear, be
wise to enter thither. And what can be enclosed
within this chest, which he wishes to keep secret

from me? Now I would wager six pots of pickled earth-worms that he has concealed in that the grave-clothes which he intends for his affectionate So-Sli. So-Sli, then, resolved to examine the chest forth-with. But first she went to a cage, in which was her husband's bird of good-luck, — a white-necked crow. Ho-Fi valued this bird beyond all his earthly possessions: he had made it tame, and had attached it to him; and he considered, that, whilst he possessed it, no material ill-fortune could befall him. So-Sli frequently fed it, and it had become fond of her also, from which it was to be believed that its kindly influence would extend to her. She took it now from its cage, and placed it on her wrist, and having tendered it a kiss, which was affectionately received and reciprocated, she went into the yard to discover the contents of the mysterious chest. She unhesitatingly raised the lid, but let it fall again with great precipitation, as, with a loud growl, a sav-age dog attempted to spring from within.

So-Sli was off with greater expedition than is fre-quently practised by the footless ladies of the Flowery Land; and the cover of the chest having fallen on the back of Bou-Wou, — such was the name of the fierce quadruped, — she was able to gain a few paces before he had struggled from beneath it.

It would soon, however, have been all over with So-Sli, — for the dog had caught a glimpse of the dress so familiar to him, and would, therefore, have mistaken his mistress for his daily bread, — had she not, with great presence of mind, seized Ho-Fi's bird of good-luck by the neck, and, whisking it rapidly three times round, thrown it to her hungry pursuer. As he jumped aside to snap at this, So-Sli reached the door, and, closing it against him, secured it with several bolts.

When Ho-Fi returned, So-Sli told him that a savage dog had got loose in the court, and that his bird of good-luck had disappeared.

"As I looked in the cage," she said, "suddenly I beheld him wax paler and paler, till, having become thinner than mist, he passed between the bars ; and what became of him after I cannot at all tell."

Ho-Fi was inconsolable for the loss of his bird. "Better," said he, "to lose nine wives than to lose a bird of good-luck." And inwardly he feared lest the bird of good-luck having thus evaporated in the presence of So-Sli might indicate the calamity he most dreaded, — that he should lose no more wives.

In a few days, however, his invention was again in active exercise. Perceiving that So-Sli's suspicions were awakened, he judged it best to send his dog back to the place in which he had been trained; and he would not try a fresh experiment with him.

Another week had passed: it was evening, and the shadows of the western hills were gradually extending eastward over the richly-cultivated fields. We mention this, not as necessary to the elucidation of our story, but merely because an erroneous opinion seems to have possessed the minds of many, that shadows are unknown in China. The artists of the Celestial Empire exhibit their hopeful character by omitting the dark side of every picture. They would make you believe that Peter Schlemihl's friend had walked through the land, and bought shadow and shade, every inch of the commodity. Foreigners, however, have not discovered that Nature, in this particular, has framed for China laws different from those in operation over other portions of the globe. But the Chinese seem really unaware that shadow exists among them; and in their writings and discourse, as in their pictures, always represent their country as an all-enlightened land.

It was evening; and the beautiful So-Sli was sitting in a veranda, very diligently engaged in embroidering a dress, and chewing betel, when Ho-Fi approached, and, assuming an appearance of sudden alarm and solicitude, exclaimed, —

"By the pig-tail and thumb-nails of Confuttsze, explain to me what ails my ever sweetest So-Sli! What sudden and malevolent disease is endeavoring to pick the lock of my casket of a thousand jewels? Your complexion, sweet mouse of my bosom, is like silk; your eyes are as dull as a stewed shark's fin; and I see well that you must be under the feeble influence of the melancholic Saturn: thence cold has gained a predominancy over heat in your temperament, and dryness over moisture. Go, therefore, to your chamber; avoid all yellow objects, and also those of gloomy white; you had better, indeed, put out your lantern, and close your window, that you may see nothing but a lively black about you. I will go hence, lest the hue of my girdle exercise a malignant effect upon you; and, if you will betake yourself to bed, I will send hither a physician of great skill, who will feel your pulses, and determine from the stars what medicines you should use."

The Chinese possess many secrets of physical

science quite unknown to the philosophers of Europe. Among others is the mysterious dependence of particular colors upon particular planets ; yellow upon Saturn, for example, and black upon Mercury. White is their mourning color ; and black, as its opposite, must needs, therefore, be regarded among them as having a particularly gay and agreeable character.

A Chinese physician is not content with feeling one pulse of his patient : he must feel many. From each he learns somewhat of the disease ; and he needs no other indications to guide him. It is a simple plan, and removes most of the difficulties that beset the European doctor in the formation of his diagnosis : pulse with him is every thing ; like the Brahmin, he lives upon pulse. He consults, indeed, the planets, as we did some centuries since ; but in one thing he resembles our modern pharmacopœists, — that beyond all stars he believes in the healing virtues of Mercury.

So-Sli wondered what the solicitude of her husband might portend. Was Bou-Wou awaiting her in her chamber, and preparing a dose of bark? "You don't bite me so easily," thought So-Sli; and she entreated Ho-Fi, that, if she should betake herself to bed, he would retire to rest at the same time. He excused himself on the ground that he must forthwith call a physician ; and though for a while she made some objections to this, — having ever entertained a great dislike to doctor's stuff and doctor's learning, which she classed together as stuff and nonsense, she could not but give in at last, as he insisted upon it with all the earnestness of affectionate solicitude.

Ho-Fi accordingly went to seek the physician ; and So-Sli taking a lantern, and having glanced in a mirror to assure herself, of what all along she had strongly suspected, that she was *not* so yellow as silk, and that her eyes were not so dull as a stewed shark's fin, proceeded to her chamber, and, very cautiously opening the door, threw in a bone before she would enter to find if the coast were clear.

As no dog snapped at the bone, So-Sli felt sufficiently assured that her canine enemy was not in the apartment. She ventured into it, therefore, but moved about with great circumspection ; and she examined the room with the utmost care, to discover *what* danger might be concealed within it ; for she had fully made up her mind that there was *some.*

She looked up the chimney ; she pryed in every

corner; she turned about the table and chairs; she looked in the oven under the bed. Yes, truly, the oven was under the bed. So to place it is the common practice in the Chinese empire, and unquestionably it is an acute plan. In one side of a chamber is an arched recess, in which is placed the bed on a raised platform, and beneath that the oven. What a very cosey thing upon a winter's night! The warming-pan as large as the mattress. You put your bread in the oven, and have a hot roll in bed; but perhaps this practice may have done something towards making the Chinese rather a crusty people.

So-Sli was not yet satisfied. "What," said she, "an' I find needles in my bed?" and the mere idea gave her a stitch in her side. She lifted the bedclothes, but let them fall again much more quickly. She was frightened; but she did not shriek. She gave utterance only to a little gasping cry, such as might proceed from a terrified "sucking dove;" and she did not run away, for, though she had arrived at womanhood, her feet were as those of an infant. However, she tottered back a few paces, and then paused to consider what she should do.

But what had she seen in the bed? Had any of

you seen it, my fair readers, the apparition of the old gentleman's tail, to which it bore a very marked resemblance, could not have frightened you more. It was a huge black adder. You must not, however, suppose, that, though startled, our little Celestial lady was scared at all in the same degree that you would have been ; by reason that she had been on most familiar terms with many of his kin in the kitchen.

So-Sli hobbled quietly out of the room. She called a female servant, and sent her into the court to bring a young rat from the coop ; to its leg they tied a small stone, and put it in a large long earthen pot with a small neck ; and, just peeping under the clothes of the bed to see whereabouts the adder lay, they thrust this in, with the mouth towards him. They listened, and after a time fancied that they heard him glide into it ; and this was confirmed by a little squeak from the rat : so, cautiously lifting the clothes, they suddenly raised the jar upon the end, and put a stopper over its mouth. The adder could not but perceive that he was rather awkwardly sit-uated. " I shall ' go to pot,' " thought he ; but it was of no use to make a coil about it.

So-Sli sat up to wait the return of her loving and

liege lord. " I shall stay by him a little yet," she said : "an adder shall not be our divider."

Two or three hours elapsed ere he came back : he had forgotten the physician.

As he entered, he seemed startled at beholding her. " My dearest So-Sli," he said, " how is it that you have not retired to bed as I requested ? "

"While you were absent from me," she answered, " how could I have rested ? I should have been haunted by dragons and demons and cockatrices. Besides, I expected to see the physician, and I was not willing that he should visit me in my bed cham- ber. How is it that he comes not with you ? "

" His own son," replied Ho-Fi, " is on the point of death, and I could not induce him to leave his bedside ; but he desired that you should not rise from your couch whilst the cold influence was upon you. He bade me spend the night in watching and fasting, and at midnight to gather certain simples on the hill without the city, from which, to-morrow, he will prepare your medicines. I conjure you then, as you love my yellow girdle, to go to bed without more delay."

So-Sli at last assented to go to bed alone ; but she would not do so until he should have partaken, with her, of a soup, which she said she had prepared for him with great care, believing that it would be agreeable to him after being so long exposed to the damp of the night. To this, so far as himself was concerned, Ho-Fi had no reasonable objection to urge; but for her sake he wished that it had not been made, and he earnestly advised her by no means to take any part thereof. The night-air had given Ho-Fi an appetite.

So-Sli promised; and they sat down on either side of a small bamboo table. A lantern was placed upon it; and the soup, introduced in a covered bowl, was put before Ho-Fi, that he might help himself. He had placed his hand upon the cover, when So-Sli accidentally knocked the lantern from the table, and the light was extinguished. She rose suddenly from her chair in great alarm, and, in doing this, upset the little table, so that the soup-bowl was thrown into the lap of Ho-Fi. Ho-Fi had on a skin apron, which he usually wore when he sat down to meals; and this he held up to catch his supper as it fell. But alack for luckless Ho-Fi! his supper caught him by the wrist, and made him roar with agony. So-Sli knew his partiality for viper-soup, but had forgotten to have the reptile *cooked.*

But So-Sli did not escape with impunity. Ho-Fi chased her around the apartment, and, driving her at last into a corner, beat her with his knotted pigtail in an unmerciful manner, until the pain of the bite he had received in his wrist made him fall down upon the floor, and grind his head against it. Whilst he was so employed, his wife stepped upon his shoulder, and, jumping over him, escaped from the house. The fright she was in gave her power to run as never before her legs had carried her, and that, too, without crutches. Fright does not always thus assist in getting us out of a *hobble.*

When the first impetus supplied by fear had abated, she assumed somewhat more of her ordinary walk. Several times she was hailed by the watchmen as she passed through the streets, but they allowed her to proceed; and at last, sorely spent with the fatigue of her long and unsupported tottering, she arrived at her father's house.

The philosopher had already retired to rest. He was angry at being thus aroused; but his indignation was beyond all bounds when he heard his daughter's story. "I will appeal," he said, "to Pekin in this matter; and we will hang Ho-Fi in his yellow girdle."

Ho-Fi, meanwhile, when the first paroxysm of pain had subsided, sent for a barber-surgeon, and had his wrist, which was swollen to the size of the calf of his leg, examined and dressed. Moreover, having, no doubt, heard of that ancient practice in chirurgery which cured the wound by anointing the weapon, he had the viper dressed also ; and revenge furnished an excellent sauce, and greatly improved his supper.

Poo-Poo, according to promise, made his appeal to the emperor. As Ho-Fi boasted his relationship to the imperial family, this was the proper course, though the local courts were not forbidden to exercise jurisdiction in similar cases. Commissioners were sent from Pekin to investigate the affair.

Ho-Fi and his wife, their domestics, Poo-Poo, and a few other persons who were required as witnesses, were summoned before the tribunal. Some of the relatives, also, of the former wives of the Yellow Girdle, took care to be present in the court.

The case was fully examined. Minute evidence was entered into to prove that Ho-Fi had in various ways attempted the life of his lady. All the circumstances connected with their marriage were set forth by Poo-Poo. So-Sli gave her evidence with **great**

15

perspicuity; and her statements respecting the poisoned tea and the fierce Bou-Wou, as well as concerning the viper in the bed, were corroborated by the testimony of the servants. Some amateur witnesses made it pretty apparent that Ho-Fi's former wives had all of them been Burked and Greenacred; and the judges and jury were fully satisfied of his guilt. The defence did not shake their confidence, though it showed that faults of less magnitude existed in some other parties. The verdict of the court having been submitted to Pekin, the following proclamation was in a few days received from the emperor, the Son of Heaven, and Father of the Celestial Empire. It was addressed to all his subjects; that is to say, to his three hundred and sixty-five millions of children.

"Pekin, the sixth month, the fourteenth day, the fifty-eighth year of the Emperor Ho-Ho.

"Unless the laws be exercised, even on the imperial kindred, they will not be obeyed.

"When the mulberry shall degenerate into the thorn, it is time that it should be rooted out.

"Guilt shall not escape the penetrating ears of Ho-Ho. Ho-Ho hath long ears.

"Ho-Ho would emulate the virtues of his father,

Ha-Ha, and train up by good example, his son He-He.

"It hath come to the knowledge of Ho-Ho, that a certain yellow girdle, namee Ho-Fi, residing in the city of Din-Din, not respecting the imperial pleasure, so often proclaimed, that all shall live peaceably together, without committing offences against their neighbors, hath contumaciously presumed to put six wives to death by various devices, and hath in like manner attempted the life of a seventh. The modes of their deaths have been these (for each he accounted falsely), — the first fell from a rock; he ascribed it to female giddiness: the second was drowned; he said that she died of drink: the third was hanged; he spoke of her tightness of breath: the fourth was poisoned; he declared she was not careful in diet: the fifth was starved; he said that she lived too low: the sixth was choked with her shoe; he gave out that she could not say herself how she died. By these evasions he for a while eluded justice; but the truth hath become manifest; the chicken hath pipped the shell; the cat can no longer conceal the kittens; the parrot hath moulted, let him be ashamed of his tail.

"But it is agreeable to the rules of justice that the punishment should bear some reference to the particular nature of the crime. This was the attempted murder of the seventh wife, which he hath essayed by poison, by a dog, and by a viper. It is the will, then, of Ho-Ho, that Ho-Fi be punished in this manner: that he be stung to death by adders, and that his heart be filled with poison, and given to the dog Bou-Wou. In consideration of his former enormities, it is farther ordered, that his body be cut into exceeding small pieces, one of which shall be sent to every square *ly* * throughout the empire, and stuck upon a thorn. That his ten nearest relatives be put to death also ; but, as it is well to temper justice with mercy, they shall be merely strangled. His wife, So-Sli, shall be stran· gled likewise. His servants shall submit each to two hundred strokes of the bamboo. Poo-Poo, the father of So-Sli, shall receive five hundred, and shall wear the wooden collar for twelve calendar months, a proper reward for his heretical doctrines. The allowance of pay and rice to all yellow girdles shall cease for three years ; and the principal mandarin of Din-Din shall be hung up in his house."

* A ly is a measure of distance about equal to our furlong.

For "hung up in his house," some versions of the proclamation read, "suspended in his office."

The wind-up of this enunciation of the Celestial will is too long for insertion here : it exhibits a fine struggle between a proper humility, and conscious wisdom.

The story of Ho-Fi is told. Chinese and poetical justice go hand in hand. His name has long been universally execrated throughout the Celestial Empire. The Greeks borrowed it ; and among them οφι was an expression equivalent to "Oh, thou serpent!" Even among us barbarous inhabitants of the isles of the Western Ocean, "Oh, fie!" is to this day used to convey a reproach.

WALTON REDIVIVUS.

A NEW RIVER ECLOGUE.

By Thomas Hood.

(PISCATOR is fishing, near the Sir Hugh Middle-ton's Head, without either basket or can. VIA-TOR cometh up to him, with an angling-rod and a bottle.)

VIA. Good-morrow, Master Piscator. Is there any sport afloat?

Pis. I have not been here time enough to answer for it. It is barely two hours agone since I put in.

Via. The fishes are shyer in this stream than in any water that I know.

Pis. I have fished here a whole Whitsuntide through without a nibble. But then the weather was not so excellent as to-day. This nice shower will set the gudgeons all agape.

Via. I am impatient to begin.

Pis. Do you fish with gut?

Via. No—I bait with gentles.

Pis. It is a good taking bait: though my question referred to the nature of your line. Let me see your tackle. Why, this is no line, but a ship's cable. It is a six-twist. There is nothing in this water but you may pull out with a single hair.

Via. What! are there no dace, nor perch?—

Pis. I doubt not that there have been such fish in former ages. But now-a-days there is nothing of that size. They are gone extinct like the mammoths.

Via. There was always such a fishing at them. Where there was one angler in former times, there is now a hundred.

Pis. A murrain on them!—A New River fish now-a-days, cannot take his common swimming exercise, without hitching on a hook.

Via. It is a natural course of things, for man's populousness to terminate other breeds. As the proverb says, "The more Scotchmen, the fewer herrings." It is curious to consider the family of whales growing thinner according to the propagation of parish lamps.

Pis. Aye, and withal, how the race of man, who is a terrestrial animal, should have been in the greatest jeopardy of extinction by the element of water; whereas the whales, living in the ocean, are most liable to be burnt out.

Via. It is a pleasant speculation. But how is this?—I thought to have brought my gentles comfortably in an old snuff-box, and they are all stark dead!

Pis. The odor hath killed them, there is nothing more mortal than tobacco, to all kinds of vermin. Wherefore, a new box will be indispensable, though for my own practice, I prefer my waistcoat pockets for their carriage. Pray, mark this:—and in the meantime I will lend you some worms.

Via. I am much beholden: and when you come to Long Acre I will faithfully repay you. But, look you, my tackle is still amiss. My float will not swim.

Pis. It is no miracle—for here is at least a good ounce of swanshots upon your line. It is overcharged with lead.

Via. I confess, I am only used to killing sparrows, and such small fowls, out of the back-casement. But my ignorance shall make me the more thankful for your help and instruction.

Pis. There. The fault is amended. And now observe,—you must watch your cork very narrowly, without even an eyewink the other way :—for other-wise, you may overlook the only nibble throughout the day.

Via. I have a bite already :—my float is going up and down like a ship at sea.

Pis. No, it is only that housemaid dipping in her bucket, which causes the agitation you perceive. 'Tis a shame so to interrupt the honest angler's diversion. It would be but a judgment of God, now, if the jade should fall in !

Via. But I should have her drowned only for some brief twenty minutes or so—and then restored again by the Surgeons. And yet I have doubts of the law-fulness of that dragging of souls back again, that have taken their formal leaves. In my conscience, it seems like flying against the laws of predestination.

Pis. It is a doubtful point ;—for, on the other hand, I have heard of some that were revived into life by the Doctors, and came afterwards to be hanged.

Via. Marry ! 'tis a pity such knaves' lungs were ever puffed up again. It was good tobacco-smoke ill-wasted. Oh ! how pleasant, now, is this angling, which furnishes us with matter for such agreeable discourse ! Surely it is well called a contemplative recreation, for I never had half so many thoughts in my head before !

Pis. I am glad you relish it so well.

Via. I will take a summer lodging hereabouts, to be near the stream. How pleasant is this solitude ! There are but fourteen a-fishing here—and of those but few men.

Pis. And we shall be still more lonely on the other side of the City Road. Come, let's across. Nay, we'll put in our lines lower down. There was a butcher's wife dragged for at this bridge in the last week.

Via. Have, you, indeed, any qualms of that kind ?

Pis. No, but hereabouts 'tis likely the gudgeons will be gorged. Now, we are far enough. Yonder is the row of Colebrook. What a balmy, wholesome gust is blowing over to us from the cow-lair.

Via. For my part, I smell nothing but dead kittens—for here lies a whole brood in soak. Would you believe it, to my fantasy, the nine days' blindness of these creatures smacks somewhat of the type of the human pre-existence. Methinks, I have had myself such a mysterious being before I beheld the light—my dreams hint of it. A sort of world before eye sight.

Pis. I have some dim sympathy with your meaning.   At the creation, there was such a kind of blind-man's-buff work.   The atoms jostled together, be-fore there was a revealing sun.   But are we not fish-ing too deep?

Via. I am afraid on't !   Would we had a plummet. We shall catch weeds.

Pis. It would be well to fish thus at the bottom, if we were fishing for flounders in the sea.   But there you must have forty fathom, or so, of stout line ; and then, with your fish at the end, it will be the boy's old pastime carried into another element. I assure you, 'tis like swimming a kite.

Via. It should be pretty sport—but hush !   My cork has just made a bob.   It is diving under the water !—Hallo !—I have catched a fish !

Pis. Is it a great one?

Via. Purely, a large one !   Shall I put it into the bottle ?

Pis. It will be well,—and let there be a good measure of water too, lest he scorch against the glass.

Via. How slippery and shiny it is !   Ah, he is gone !

Pis. You are not used to the handling of a New River fish ; and indeed very few be.   But hath he altogether escaped ?

Via. No, I have his chin here, which I was obliged to tear off, to get away my hook.

Pis. Well, let him go ; it would be labor wasted to seek for him amongst this rank herbage. 'Tis the commonest of anglers' crosses.

Via. I am comforted to consider he did not fall into the water again, as he was without a mouth, and might have pined for years. Do you think there is any cruelty in our art ?

Pis. As to other methods of taking fish, I cannot say : But I think none in the hooking of them. For, to look at the gills of a fish, with those manifold red leaves—like a housewife's needle-book,—they are admirably adapted to our purpose, and manifestly intended by nature to stick our steel in.

Via. I am glad to have the question so comfortably resolved—for, in truth, I have had some misgivings. Now, look how dark the water grows I There is another shower towards.

Pis. Let it come down, and welcome. I have only my working-day clothes on. Sunday coats spoil holidays. Let everything hang loose, and time, too, will sit easy.

Via. I like your philosophy. In this world we are the fools of restraint. We starch our ruffs till they cut us under the ear.

Pis. How pleasant it would be to discuss these

sentiments over a tankard of ale! I have a simple bashfulness against going into a public tavern ; but I think we could dodge into the Castle without being much seen.

Via. And I have a sort of shuddering about me that is willing to go more frankly in. Let us put up, then. By my halidom! here is a little dead fish hanging at my hook, and yet I have never felt him bite.

Pis. 'Tis only a little week-old gudgeon, and he had not strength enough to stir the cork. However, we may say boldly that we have caught a fish.

Via. Nay, I have another here in my bottle. He was sleeping on his back at the top of the water, and I got him out nimbly with the hollow of my hand.

Pis. We have caught a brace, then,—besides the great one that was lost among the grass. I am glad on't, for we can bestow them on some poor hungry person in our way home. It is passable good sport for the place.

Via. I am satisfied it must be called so. But the next time I come, I shall bring a reel with me, and a newly-made minnow, for I am certain there must be some marvellous huge pikes here ; they always

make a scarcity of other fish.   However, I have
been bravely entertained, and at the first holiday, I
will come to it again.

FINIS.